RISARIAL

HOLLY THORNE

CHAPTER 1

Risarial wended her away across the ridgeline, booted feet clacking loudly on the paved path. The moon was full, licking at the edges of wispy clouds and vying with the dome of light emanating from the city at the base of the ridge.

She had waited for the moon, needing its benignant light to guide her to the cluster of boulders she sought tonight. The way they loomed up against the light-polluted sky reminded her of a slumbering dragon, a relic from a world mostly forgotten. Risarial smiled wryly. She was from that world too.

She came across the first of the stones and slowly picked her way over them, frowning each time her long black gown caught under her feet—she couldn't wait to be rid of the damn thing. Her keen eyes found the gash in the boulder she'd made using a pen knife stolen on one of her trips. Hunkering down, she regarded the base of the boulder before rolling up her sleeves and beginning to dig. Slowly, she unearthed an array of objects—a large duffel bag, a plastic sheaf with a mobile phone and charger coiled inside, and another packed full of human money. Risarial sneered at the last item—that, she certainly wouldn't need.

Unzipping the duffel bag with dirt-blackened fingers, Risarial pulled out a few neatly folded items of clothing and stood up to remove her dress. For a while, she stood naked in the light of the moon, gazing down at the city of Manchester huddled at the bottom of the vast hills she walked upon. It looked so small from here; quiet, sleepy, though she knew it was anything but.

She pulled on a pair of jeans and a black long-sleeved shirt. Running her hands over the cotton, she allowed herself to reminisce on the last time she wore these clothes.

When the memories just as quickly soured, she set her jaw and kicked her dress into a heap beneath the boulder. The action reminded her of a human funeral as she heaped soil back on top of it, and she only hoped that signified new beginnings and wasn't a portent of doom.

ঌৎ

Risarial stepped up into Parsonage Gardens, eyes fixed on the building at the end of the small green. The block of flats was all rust-coloured brick and stylish blue glass and interior lights made to imitate sunlight. Risarial didn't think it held a candle to the grand Edwardian buildings nestled up to its side, but apparently the modern flats were rented out at ridiculous prices and eagerly lapped up by the humans who leased them.

She stepped up to the door and keyed in a code, shaking her head when it immediately beeped her through. The idiot hadn't even thought to change the numbers.

She took the lift to the top floor, enjoying the whooshing feeling in her stomach as it zoomed upwards. She regarded herself in the mirror, her reflection stark beneath the fluorescent lights. Glossy black hair tumbled over her breasts, framing a long, oval face which always reminded her of her mother, no matter how much she glamoured herself. Her eyes were dark, almost black, and her lips were red though she wore no colour. A snippet of a memory flooded her mind. *You always look like you've just been kissed,* came the teasing voice, a voice which made her smile as she continued her scrutiny, running her eyes down her denim-clad legs.

She always wondered what humans thought of her when they looked at her and she wondered even more how they'd react if she showed them her true form.

The lift finally opened onto a white corridor, devoid of residents at this hour but full of traces of them—doormats and scuffs on the floor from numerous feet and the odd coffee cup which would be swiped by the cleaners tomorrow. The apartment she sought was right at the end, tucked into a little alcove.

Risarial put a hand in her back pocket, fingers closing around a key, the metal warm from her body. Then she retracted it, raising a hand to knock instead. A smirk formed on her lips—she wanted to see the shock in his face at seeing her here.

The door opened. Risarial smiled deeper, an eyebrow rising as the man's silence ticked on. He was still dressed in his work suit, shoes on, tie loosened and lying askew around his neck. His face was slack with horror.

'No,' he finally breathed.

'Yes, you snivelling rat.'

Risarial stepped forward and moved him out the way, hand braced on his chest. She stood in the middle of the open-planned apartment, eyes roving over the familiar cool-coloured walls and low furniture, the lights hanging over the kitchen island and the LED waterfall feature which glowed pleasantly beside the panoramic TV.

'Please,' the man said behind her. 'You can't do this to me again.'

'Shut up,' she snapped, letting her glamour fall from her. Whatever protest the man was about to utter next froze in his throat as she turned back around.

He swallowed and in a hoarse voice asked, 'How long this time?'

Risarial could see sweat beading on his forehead.

'However long I wish.' She took a step towards the bedroom. 'Come on,' she beckoned.

'Please,' he begged again. 'I'm seeing my daughter tomorrow. It's her birthday. I can't—'

Risarial reached out, grabbed the man by his arm and

shoved him into the bedroom. He stopped outside the walk-in wardrobe and turned back to her beseechingly.

She nodded at the door. 'In.'

Sobbing now, the man walked into the wardrobe and towards the rail at the back that housed all of his executive blazers. He staggered back, shouldering his way between two jackets.

Closing her eyes to his tears, Risarial raised a hand and ran it over the man's face, careful not to touch any of that dirty wet skin. When she finally looked up, he was slumped, staring into space with a stupid grin on his stupid face. Risarial grimaced at the patch of wet trickling from his trouser leg. Turning, she exited the wardrobe, closing the door firmly behind her.

She looked around the bedroom, lip curling at the state of the rumpled bedsheets and underwear strewn across the carpet. Releasing a sigh, she bent down, plucking a pair of boxers between pinched fingers. Throwing them into the laundry hamper, she turned to a rogue sock and did the same. She would move to the kitchen next and she wouldn't stop until the place was immaculate.

CHAPTER 2

It had grown cold. Before leaving the flat again, Risarial took a coat hidden at the back of the wardrobe. It was a woman's coat. The man—Matthew or Michael or whatever his name was—had been married once and there were a few mementos still dotted around the place. It was pitiful really.

Sliding her hands into the deep pockets of the tan-coloured trench coat, Risarial walked back through the gardens. It was past midnight now and the place lay quiet. Heading west, she crossed the bridge over the river, taking a second to gaze into it. A nixie bobbed just below the surface, humming gently. A human couple stood at the bridge's edge, staring into the water. Though they couldn't hear the nixie's song, they were still compelled to stop and peer down.

Spotting Risarial with its large bulbous eyes, it nodded its head once before descending back into the depths. The human couple roused and continued their night walk. Briefly, Risarial wondered what choices the nixie had made to wind up here, swimming in the filth of a polluted city river.

She was soon on Chapel Street, the buildings lining it wrapped in scaffolding, the walls below tagged heavily in graffiti. She turned off onto a quieter lane, slowing her steps when she found the building she wanted. Looking around, she couldn't see anyone. She only hoped she was early and not too late. For the first time since arriving earthside,

Risarial felt a welling of nerves. She stepped back into the shadow of a large bin and waited.

�� ��

At exactly ten past one, the girl emerged from around the corner. Risarial leant her head further back, out of the light of the streetlamp and watched. The girl fiddled around in her bag, searching for her key. She looked just as Risarial remembered, dressed in all black, like Risarial herself usually was; something they'd bonded over the first time they'd met. She wore a light leather jacket and her hair was just as short as the last time she'd seen her. Risarial let out a slow breath through her nose, blood tingling at the sight of this human. Part of her loathed that such a creature could have this effect on her. A bigger part, though, yearned to be recognised.

Just as the girl put the key into the door, Risarial stepped out of the shadows.

'Ruth.'

The girl looked over her shoulder. Her eyes remained blank, even as they connected with hers, but the sudden spike in the girl's heartrate made Risarial's nostrils flare. It almost made her sway.

Then Ruth laughed. 'Are you actually fucking kidding me?'

'Ruth, just listen.'

'No.' Ruth turned back to the door and opened it. 'Fuck off.'

Gritting her teeth, Risarial reached out and pulled Ruth around to face her.

'Listen to me,' she implored.

Ruth sighed, shucking Risarial's hand from her and folding her arms. 'What?'

Risarial wetted her lips. 'Ruth,' she began, voice low, 'I...despise how I left things. I've returned to...make amends. With you.'

Ruth scoffed lightly. 'What, just like that? Really? And you didn't just leave things. You majorly fucked them up.'

'I know.'

'No.' Ruth shook her head. 'I don't think you actually do. You don't have any idea what you—' Ruth released a breath, her eyes going to somewhere above Risarial's head. When she looked back, her expression was shuttered again. 'I'm seeing someone else now. I'm not interested in anything you have to say. So you can take your grovelling and fucking do one.'

A dark, black feeling slithered up Risarial's body. 'What?'

'I said I'm with someone else now.' She turned back towards the door. 'She's coming over in a minute and she'll kick your face in if she sees you here.'

She walked through the door, reaching a palm back to slam it shut. Much as she'd done that man, Risarial shouldered her way in after her, backing Ruth up against the wall. She looked into Ruth's eyes. They were green now in the dingy light of the entryway. Outside, just then, they'd been grey.

'Get off me,' Ruth whispered.

Risarial debated for only a second before leaning her forehead against Ruth's and closing her eyes. 'Forgive me,' she breathed before running a hand over the girl's face, murmuring a spell. This time, she let her fingers stroke the soft, warm skin. Ruth slumped in her arms. Risarial caught her and looked down the entryway.

'Come on,' she murmured, holding the girl tightly as they shuffled their way down the corridor. The girl moaned quietly and Risarial soothed her with a hand to the forehead. Ruth's key had fallen onto the threadbare carpet. Risarial picked it up and unlocked the flat door.

She led Ruth to the sofa. She removed her boots, rightened her jacket where it had rucked up beneath her and prized off all the silver stacking rings from her fingers. Beneath the jacket, Ruth wore her black work shirt. She had been working at the pub, just as Risarial had predicted.

Getting to her knees, Risarial stroked a hand over the girl's forehead, pushing back her hair.

'I vow,' she whispered, voice trembling, 'this time will be different. The next time we meet, I'll just be a stranger to you and we'll start again. We'll start right from the beginning again, okay?'

Risarial battled down a wave of grief that this girl wouldn't remember her anymore—not the tenor of her voice, their shared, secret smiles; she wouldn't remember how their bodies moulded nor all the ways they'd talked without speaking. Ruth wouldn't even know her name.

Risarial hadn't meant for it to go like this but she couldn't see another way. She took a breath before finishing, 'You will cease all relations with this other person and you will never speak to them again.'

After hovering for another moment, drinking in the gentle, sleep-softened slopes of the girl's face, Risarial pressed a kiss to her head.

'Until the night we meet again.'

CHAPTER 3

On the sofa the girl twitched, sending her rings clattering over the coffee table. The streetlight outside the window shone on the tears pooling at her temples.

Slowly, torturously, the memories leaked from her like heavy metallic oil sluicing down a drain. Before they faded, they played in a cruel reel, the ticking loud in her mind.

The night they met: a beat deep and heavy sounding from the speakers by the stage. A festival. The day just cooling, the sky dusky. Ruth turned in the sea of people and saw her. Instead of her eyes being on the stage, this girls' were up on the sky and they were closed. Ruth took a step towards her and the memory fell away.

There was skin, pale and white and moving slickly to a beat only they could hear. Dark hair finger-raked and messy. Spots of pink on their cheeks and chests. Contented smiles and exhausted kisses and then a severing which made her beg. A severing which cut her soul.

There was the smashing of glass and loud silence and the angry, flashing of eyes. A quick burst of flame and then a dousing of water. They came together again; that was their way. It was an addiction and Ruth cried out, her drug forced from her.

Then there were monsters all around her. Cat-eared women and green-painted men. She sobbed in her slumber. Not this night—she couldn't bear this night. The end of them, the end of herself. She turned away from them and though her mouth was closed, she was screaming.

Ruth lost her many times in the dark. So many nights spent intertwined, in beds and at clubs and the cool darkness of cinemas. It didn't matter that she couldn't see her, Ruth could always feel her. But she couldn't now. That darkness was empty.

Tears turning to sand on her cheeks, Ruth stilled. She turned to her side, tucked her hands under a cushion and breathed out. The reel ticked to a stop. Ruth leaned into the darkness and slept.

CHAPTER 4

The bus was rocking her to sleep. Ruth yawned and widened her bleary eyes as they gazed out at the warehouses and old bricked up buildings they passed. The bus began to slow and Ruth got up to jostle her way down the centre aisle, making sure the camera bag slung over her shoulder didn't nick anyone.

She murmured a thanks to the driver and hopped down onto the pavement. The bus drove off in a cloud of fumes and Ruth blew out a breath, waving a hand in front of her face before starting off down the street.

She came to the shutter of the boarded up building she wanted—an old cutlery factory that the council was going to demolish to make room for some fancy flats. Ruth slowed her steps and looked around. Across the road from her, a man in hi-vis coveralls sat outside a building site, eating a sandwich from a nearby eatery and scrolling through his phone. Ruth leant back against the wall beside the shutter and pulled her camera out of its bag. She'd have to wait for him to piss off first.

She scrolled through her photos—of old buildings she'd visited, of her work friends at the last party she'd had with them at her flat, of Sheila sitting in her trusty armchair, ashtray at her elbow—whilst sneaking glances at the construction worker. As soon as he'd stood up and turned away, Ruth bagged up the camera and slipped beneath the shutter. She was surprised they were still open. Her urbexing forum had spotted the opening a few days ago and she'd been sceptical on the bus ride over.

Inside, she took a moment to scan over the factory floor, on the lookout for other people who might be sharing the space with her. They were usually teenagers or urban explorers like her but a few times she'd startled people in the middle of an obvious drug drop. They were never pleased to see her but she always managed to blag her way out of the situation by saying she was a photography student. For some reason, that always set them at ease.

Fortunately, she couldn't see anyone today. The floor was a mess of rubble and rusty metal and smeary, sooty windows. Ruth could see the shadows of people on the other side of them. She unbagged her camera again and took a picture, zooming in on the anonymous figures.

Carefully, she walked to the centre of the room and looked up through the vast gap in the ceiling. The factory reached up, floor after floor, but Ruth couldn't see access to any stairs. She tilted her head back and raised her camera, the click sounding loudly through the building.

She walked around slowly. There was a metal support along one of the edges, the thick paint peeling off it in chunks, the metal underneath a deep orange. A heart had been rashly spray painted onto it, a couple of initials scrawled below. Someone had come along afterwards and severed the heart with an angry black line.

Ruth snorted softly. She felt a bit like that today, remembering the disbelief and hurt on Molly's face when she'd broken up with her in the small hours of the morning. She hadn't even given her the chance to set down the pizza she'd been carrying. It sat on her table now, cold and untouched and stinking up her flat with garlic.

Every time she thought she should feel guilty, the feeling was whisked away by a hard knowing that she'd done the right thing. She couldn't be sure why, things had been pretty good before that, but she'd woken up from that impromptu nap on the sofa with a gnawing in her gut which wouldn't go away—not until Molly had.

Ruth thumbed the scroll wheel on her camera uneasily. It was bound to make things awkward at work. Molly was the pub's cleaner—it was how they'd met—and Ruth often saw her in the mornings when she was on the open. Sheila was probably going to be pissed about that, especially if the girl jacked in her job because of it. Ruth wouldn't blame her if she did. Maybe she did feel a little bit guilty, remembering just how many times Molly had asked *why?* and not being able to give an answer.

'You're a proper dick, Ruth,' she murmured.

'Talking to yourself?'

Ruth's head snapped up, spotting the man standing behind her with a wry grin on his face and a camera held at his chest. Ruth sagged back against the crumbling support and glared. 'Fucking hell Jed, you scared the shit out of me!'

Jed laughed. 'You should be keeping your wits about you, girl. I wasn't trying to be quiet.' The man moved her so he could take a picture of the broken heart. He pointed at it when he was done. 'Love. Humanity's curse.'

'Don't need to tell me twice.'

She followed him along the rim of the room, eyes on the skull tattooed on the back of his bald head. He had a flower sneaking up the left side of his neck and a tiny cross beneath one of his eyes. He was still pretty scary to look at, even after knowing him for all this time.

'How long you been here?' he asked.

'Not long. Just got here.'

'Be a shame to see it go,' he murmured, photographing the ceiling just as she had.

Ruth nodded, kicking at a rusty spoon and sending it skidding across the floor. She was remembering the scar running along her side, the one she'd gotten at some abandoned brewery. It was after a gnarly accident involving a barbed wire fence that she and Jed had become tentative friends. Turned out he ran the urbexing forum Ruth frequented online. He was the one who encouraged Ruth to post her photos.

'How's it going then, lass?'

Ruth pursed her lips. 'It's going.'

Jed didn't ask her to elaborate. That was one of the things she liked about him the most. He was quiet and didn't really give a shit about other people and their problems. But he would walk with her and take pictures with her and she knew he'd help her out of a scrape in a flash.

'How about you?' she asked.

'Yeah, you know.'

Ruth smiled behind her camera. They'd probably had their fill of conversation now. She let the silence settle comfortably over them, ears picking up on the ghostly noises of people on the pavements outside, the wind rustling through old newspapers strewn about the place, and the odd bat of a pigeon's wings from where they roosted in the rafters.

At the far end of the room was a door. It was pretty jammed, Ruth knew she wouldn't have been able to get through on her own, but Jed managed to shoulder his way in, falling to his knees in the room beyond.

Ruth reached down to help him up. 'Alright mate?'

Jed nodded, brushing off his dusty knees. The room they stood in now was a veritable kaleidoscope compared to the one they'd just left. Colourful graffiti was sprayed onto every available surface, most of it your regular tags and dicks, but some were painted by obviously talented street artists.

In the middle of the room, running along a huge dividing wall was the painting of a woman. Her eyes were at half-slit; Ruth couldn't work out if she was supposed to be dead or alive. Her russet hair fanned around her, some tendrils wrapping around her neck like coiled snakes. There was blood pooling from her mouth and over her lips. A huge stain of it was on the floor below too and Ruth wondered if that was deliberate or just some accident the artist had made the best of.

Jed grunted as he spotted it and wandered over to take some pictures.

Ruth followed. 'What is it?'

'*Dearg Due.*'

'Come again?'

Jed glanced over his shoulder. 'Fairy vampire. Irish.'

'Cool.' She raised her camera, zoomed in on the girl's dead eyes and released the shutter. 'This one real?'

'Everything's real. Monsters 'specially.'

Ruth nodded. At this point, she never tried to refute him. She'd come to enjoy his beliefs and whacky ways and his weird, esoteric knowledge. Hanging out with Jed was always a bit of a surreal adventure but she welcomed the opportunity to put down her boring life for a while.

She took one more picture of the fairy vampire before moving on to the next room.

CHAPTER 5

Risarial was at the kitchen window, looking down at two human boys kissing in the gardens when a knock sounded at the door. She slipped back into her glamour and crossed over to open it.

A child stood there, a big smile on her face which slowly faded the more Risarial frowned at her.

'Yes?' Risarial said.

'Where's my daddy?' the girl asked shyly, peeking around Risarial.

'He's not here.'

'Oh.' The girl stared at her, playing with the toggles on her rain jacket. 'When will he be back?'

'A long time. He's…he's away with work.'

The girl frowned. 'No.'

'Yes. He won't be back today. He's terribly sorry. Now, run along back to where you came from.' Risarial reached out and pushed at the girl's shoulder.

The girl resisted. 'Mummy's gone. She drove away. Daddy is supposed to be in.'

Risarial sighed. As she racked her mind of ways to get rid of the aggravating thing, the girl took a step forward.

'Are they my presents?'

Risarial glanced over her shoulder. An assortment of boxed toys and plushies lay there, some wrapped up, but most of them not. A roll of pink wrapping paper lay next to the pile, along with a reel of Sellotape and a pair of scissors.

She'd kicked it all to the side in her haste to tidy the place.

'They must be.'

The girl ducked under her arm, skidding to her knees beside the pile. 'He didn't wrap them,' she lamented, reaching out to touch a toy horse. There were stars printed on its hide and its mane was pink.

Risarial let the door click shut. She took a couple of slow steps towards the girl and stood over her, arms crossed. 'What do you think you're doing?'

The girl peeked up at her. 'Should I have waited until they were wrapped up first?'

'You should have waited until you were invited in.'

The girl pulled the horse onto her lap and clutched it tight. 'Who are you?'

'Never mind that.' Risarial leaned down slightly, peering into the girl's eyes. 'Who are you?'

'Olivia,' she replied. 'Are you Daddy's girlfriend?'

Risarial laughed. 'I think not.'

Olivia peered around the flat. 'His cleaner?' Risarial snorted. 'Is he really not here?' The girl looked sad. 'He forgot my birthday.'

Risarial kicked at a cuddly elephant. 'He obviously didn't.' She looked at the presents still wrapped. 'Well? Aren't you going to open the rest?'

Nodding dully, the girl pulled another toy onto her lap. Risarial watched her pick carefully at the tape and fold the paper back up neatly. After a couple of minutes she had an array of things laying in front of her—coloured pens, a book to go with them, a plastic glittery microphone. She didn't seem excited about any of it.

'What age are you today, youngling?' asked Risarial. She'd taken a seat on the low sofa and watched with her chin propped up on a fist.

'Eight,' the girl replied.

'So darlingly young,' Risarial murmured. She was a little thing, with olive skin and large dark eyes. Her hair was black and shiny, pulled back into two ponytails. The Gentry ladies

20

would adore her. If she didn't have other business here tonight, she'd think about taking her back with her and gifting the child to them.

'Two years and I'll be ten.' Olivia pulled the horse to her again. It was clearly the most favourite of all the toys.

'Hm.'

After a while, the girl began to stare again. Risarial frowned. 'What?'

'Are we going out?'

'Going out where?'

'Daddy said he'd take me for a milkshake at Magic Shakes. He said I could get the big chocolate one this time. Last time I had it I was sick all in the car on the way to the cinema but I promised not to be sick this time.'

Risarial curled her lip at the image. She sat up straight, thinking. She could stuff the girl in the wardrobe with her father but then she'd have a mother banging at the door soon enough and the thought of housing a whole family of glamoured humans—Risarial sighed. It was enough to give her a headache. She much preferred it last time when the man was estranged from his family.

Rubbing her forehead, she asked, 'Where is this eatery?'

'Magic Shakes?' The girl jumped up. 'Not far. I know the way. I can show you if you don't know it.'

Nodding reluctantly, Risarial let Olivia lead her way back to the door.

'Can we take the lift?' the girl shouted, skipping down the corridor. She stopped outside it and stabbed at the button multiple times. 'Quick, it's coming. I can hear it.'

The doors rolled open and they stepped inside.

'Down to the bottom,' the girl sang, pressing the correct button.

As the lift descended, Risarial looked at the two of them in the mirror. With their dark eyes and hair, Risarial wondered if people would think they were parent and child. Reaching out, she ran a hand over one of the girl's ponytails.

It turned out the milkshake joint was only a stone's

throw away from the flat. The girl bounded away from her when she spotted it and disappeared inside. When Risarial caught up, she'd taken a seat on a high booth and sat kicking her legs, scrutinising the menu.

'This is the one I want,' she said, jabbing a finger at the laminated paper. She glanced up as Risarial slid onto the booth opposite her. 'Do you have money?'

She didn't. Risarial rolled her eyes and patted around on the booth until her fingers caught the edges of a crumpled receipt. She pulled it onto her lap and ran a palm over it. When she flicked it onto the table a moment later, the girl saw nothing but a ten-pound note. She smiled and nodded happily.

'What are you getting?' Olivia pushed the menu across the table. Risarial saw splatters of crusty chocolate sauce and numerous fingerprints. She grimaced and used one finger to push it back.

'Nothing for me.'

The girl pouted but didn't argue. After a moment, she peeked up at Risarial. 'Aren't you going to get it for me, then?'

Risarial looked around. There was a boy in a ridiculous bubble gum pink top and trousers taking the order of a table nearby. One glance from Risarial and he was plodding his way over, a silly smile on his face. Risarial gestured at the girl and sat back while she ordered.

'So, why are you in my daddy's house?' Olivia sucked on her milkshake. The concoction was so thick, the girl's cheeks pinkened at the exertion. 'Are you there to clean? Mummy said he could do with it.'

Risarial pursed her lips. 'I'm on a little holiday,' she said. 'I'm going to be using your father's apartment for a time.'

She crinkled her nose. 'Holiday in Manchester? Why?'

Why indeed. 'A long time ago,' she began, fingers absently playing with the loose change from the milkshake order, 'I once met someone here. We became close. And then…and then things got bad and I went back home without ever

22

resolving things.'

'You mean a boy?' Olivia lowered her voice to a whisper. 'A boy you liked?'

Risarial shook her head. She too whispered, 'A girl.'

Olivia nodded sagely. 'What's her name?'

'Ruth.'

The girl repeated the name quietly to herself. 'And now you want to make things better with her?'

Risarial nodded. 'Exactly that.'

'What are you going to do?'

'What do you think I should do?'

Olivia frowned. 'Well, sometimes Daddy gets Mummy flowers when he thinks she's mad with him. You could try that but I don't know what girls get girls.' Olivia shrugged. 'Maybe just say sorry. That's how me and Angela make friends again. She's my best friend from school. Sometimes best friend. Sometimes I like Scotia more. She's not bossy like Angela is.'

Risarial smiled. 'Maybe I'll try that then.'

Olivia nodded, slurping her milkshake loudly. Her legs swung wildly under the table. Risarial closed her eyes every time a foot made contact with her knee. 'Where are the toilets?' the girl asked. 'I forgot from last time.'

Risarial pointed towards them with a finger and the girl got up, disappearing around the wall. Leaning back, Risarial ran her eyes over the milkshake joint. There were a couple of young children with their families but mostly the place was full of teenagers. Loud teenagers, a couple of them ogling her. Risarial stared back until they looked away.

When Olivia returned, she slipped back onto the booth and asked, 'So when are you seeing Ruth?'

'Tonight.'

'But I'm supposed to be sleeping over,' Olivia protested. A little of her earlier sadness returned. 'That was my birthday plan.'

Risarial drew in a slow breath, the whine in the girl's voice rankling her. This was getting tiring now. She needed the child gone but maybe…maybe another day's grace wouldn't hurt. It would give her more time to think about how she was going to approach things.

'Tomorrow then.'

The girl nodded. 'Tomorrow.'

Later that night, when the sky had darkened and a light rain fell over the city, Risarial sat up straight on the sofa, blue light shining over her from the large telly. The girl's head was in her lap and she stroked the soft hair absentmindedly, the strands now loose from their ponytails.

She wasn't sure what they were watching. Some surreal animation involving jungle animals. TVs had been a source of fascination for her the first time she'd come earthside. The very first one she'd come across had been inside a shop and she'd pressed her fingers to it, prodding at the staticky glass until a member of staff warded her away. Visiting a cinema was still one of her favourite earthly things to do. There she could take off her glamour and sit in the dark and slurp from tangy, fizzy slushies.

She decided, if things went well, she'd take Ruth to one again. She knew Ruth liked dark places too.

'I'm bored.'

Risarial paused in her stroking as Olivia rolled over onto her back, looking up at her.

'I thought you were asleep,' said Risarial.

The girl screwed up her face. 'I wasn't sleeping.'

'Well, what would you like to do?'

The girl shrugged.

Sighing, Risarial looked over the open-planned, minimalist apartment. It wasn't exactly fitted out for a young child's entertainment.

'Why don't you go down into the garden?'

The girl frowned. 'It's dark and it's raining.'

'So?'

The girl folded her arms, still frowning

'You're a petulant little thing.' Pushing the child from her lap, Risarial stretched her arms above her head then

24

glanced back with a gleam of something in her eyes. 'I can show you something. If you like.'

'Yeah?'

'Yes, but you mustn't scream or be scared. You're a brave girl, aren't you Olivia?'

The girl nodded but shuffled a few inches up the sofa away from her.

Risarial used the remote to switch off the telly, leaving them dowsed in only the pale light from the LED waterfall. She closed her eyes momentarily, relishing the tingling relief as she half stripped herself from her glamour. Turning to the girl, she rolled up one of her sleeves and bared the skin of her forearm.

Olivia squealed. 'You have leaves under your skin!' She reached out and touched Risarial's arm, yanking it back when one of the leaves moved. 'Does it hurt?'

Risarial chuckled. 'No, little one.' She flexed her hand, making the black leaves and vines ripple under her skin.

'What is it? How?'

'I am not like you, Olivia. I am of a different ilk. We dwell below you, where there is no electricity or cars or shopping centres.'

'What is there?' The girl took hold of Risarial's arm and watched the foliage move raptly.

Risarial smiled slightly. 'There is rain and fruit and revels which never end, and magic and monsters and children like you, who live there and will never age.'

Olivia dropped her arm. 'But no Ruth.'

Risarial moved her eyes to the window, watching the rain sluice down the panes. 'No. There is no Ruth.'

❧ ❦

The morning light shone on the small bowl of cereal Risarial held in her hands. The small, torus-shaped pieces were all colours of the rainbow. She fished out another green one and placed it upon her tongue. Olivia had teased her for her lack of milk but Risarial had silenced her with a glare. Now the girl sat at the dining table, heartily spooning up her breakfast.

A loud ringing suddenly sounded through the flat, making Risarial wince.

'That's Mummy!' The girl jumped up and crossed over to the intercom, standing on her tiptoes. 'She rings up so she doesn't have to see Daddy.'

Risarial stepped up behind her and peered at the blurry video of the girl's mother. Her hair was dark and long. A gust of wind blew some strands into her face and she pushed them back with an impatient hand. Her face looked pinched.

'I have to go now,' Olivia said, turning to her.

Risarial nodded. Hastily, she shoved the girl's new toys into a plastic bag and thrust them at her. She leaned down, pulling the girl close. 'Now, you had a lovely time with your father for your birthday, didn't you?' The girl nodded slowly. 'You opened your presents and had a milkshake with him and afterwards you and he watched a film. And I was never here, was I?' The girl shook her head, eyes filmed over. Risarial patted her on the shoulder and gave her a little push towards the door. 'Good. Now away with you.'

CHAPTER 6

Ruth was early to work. She stepped through the open double doors of the pub, gave a wave to Fiona behind the bar, then went up the two floors to Sheila's flat and knocked loudly.

The door opened a moment later

'Alright chuck?' Sheila greeted. She was dressed in her old denim shirt, the one decorated with patches of multiple rock bands.

Ruth nodded. 'You got time for a brew?'

'More like do you have time?' Sheila moved to let her past. 'Ain't you on in a bit?'

'Yeah, I'm well early though. Don't be a slave driver.'

'Alright then, your majesty. Go sit your bony arse down and I'll bring you your brew.'

Ruth moved to the small living room and took a seat on Sheila's armchair, the beaten up leather one that rocked backwards. She'd be booted off it when Sheila came back with the tea, she always was, but it was a kind of game they liked to play.

Sheila's cat Bella hopped up and rubbed up against her, purring loudly.

'Shit, you're an engine,' Ruth laughed, pulling the cat onto her lap. As it settled, she looked up at Sheila's wall of photographs hanging over the telly, eyes finding the one of her and Sheila on the first day of her job here at the pub. Even from this distance, Ruth could see how red and swollen her eyes had been.

Ruth was hardly short but Sheila towered over her, a tank of a woman with spiky silver hair, tattooed-on eye makeup and enough facial piercings to make even Ruth— someone not a stranger to the pinch of a tattoo or piercing gun—wince. She looked pretty fierce and was, if you crossed her. Ruth had witnessed that side of her more than once with the rowdy assholes the pub sometimes attracted.

Ruth kissed Bella's head, remembering the state she was in when she first came to the pub looking for a job. She was seventeen and an absolute mess following another family argument. It was the day she'd finally cut her hair short and she had been feeling herself until she had walked into the kitchen and her mum had taken one look at her and sneered, 'Look at you. God, just look at you. You're the spit of him.'

The ensuing argument wasn't much different to any of the others but she'd just broken up with her first girlfriend and delicate wasn't even the word for what she felt.

'You're too young, duck,' Sheila had told her, allowing Ruth a brief smile before putting her attention back on the till she was attending to. 'Wait 'til you're eighteen and come back, then we'll see, eh?'

Ruth remembered her hands curling to fists, squeezing against the pressure building up behind her eyelids and the roaring in her head. Ruth wasn't one for crying, unless they were the angry kind of tears, but that day she'd just had *e-fucking-nough*.

Sheila, wondering why the girl was still standing there, looked back just as Ruth's face crumpled.

'You alright, ducky?'

Ruth had shaken her head and bolted to the toilets where she proceeded to break down on the loo. She sat there gasping behind her hands until a firm knocking came to the door and then a sigh.

'Look, I'm sorry darl. I can't give you a job here. It's just the law.'

Though Sheila couldn't see, Ruth had savagely shook her

head. 'It's not just that.'

'Yeah, I figured.' The door creaked as Sheila leant against it. 'Wanna talk about it? Me being a stranger and all. Might help.'

Ruth wasn't one to spill her guts to anyone but the closed door between them and the agony in her heart had made her crack.

'Everything's just shit,' she said, harshly tugging at the toilet roll dispenser. 'My family are all fucked up and I just need to get away from them and then my fucking girlfriend broke up with me so I can't even go there.'

'Ah. Yeah, that sucks.' Sheila heaved another sigh and for a while there was only silence. 'Look,' she'd said at last. 'Maybe I can find you a little something else. Nothing glamourous. I've been doing the cleaning here myself but getting a bit sick of it if I'm honest. Just being stingy, that's my problem.' Sheila cackled.

Ruth sniffed and wiped her nose. 'Really? When would I be able to start?'

'Whenever you like. Now, you wanna come out here so I can get another look at my future employee?'

Ruth left the stall, red nose leaking and all, and Sheila had armed her with a mop and they'd done a quick turn around the pub. Ruth had never cleaned anything so thoroughly in her life but she was desperate for the job and, honestly, all the vigorous scrubbing did wonders for her anger.

Sheila had even offered her a sofa for the night, which Ruth had thought was a little weird, but she wasn't about to pass it up. Not like she had any other alternatives.

കൈ

Ruth glanced up from where she'd been surreptitiously texting on her phone, huddled against the back of the bar. A loud laugh broke out from where the patrons were clustered at their tables, waiting for the quiz to start. Ruth liked quiz nights, especially when she wasn't the one presenting them. It meant a pretty quiet night behind the bar, where she could begin clean-down early and leave earlier too.

Seeing there was no one needing her immediate attention, she rattled off one last message and pocketed her phone before heading round the bar to the toilet. She pulled out her e-cig as she sat on the loo, hoping for a small break.

The smoke tasted of strawberry. Ruth breathed it in, swirled her tongue in the smoke before breathing it all out again. The door to the toilets opened and Ruth sat up and sighed. She pocketed her e-cig again and returned to the bar.

A girl sat there now, her side profile showing a fall of black shiny hair. Ruth scooted back behind the bar and approached her.

'Hi,' she said. 'Sorry about that. Hope you haven't been waiting too long. Can I get you anything?'

The girl caught her eyes, a small smile on her lips making Ruth's lips turn up too.

'I'll have an Old Fashioned if you please,' she said, her voice smooth and low.

Ruth nodded and looked around her. 'Okay, bear with. Truth be told, next to nobody orders cocktails here so I just need to find the list thingy.'

'Take your time.'

Ruth turned her back, the tiny hairs on the back of her neck spiking as she felt the girl watching her. On the other side of the room, the quiz was underway. All was silent apart from music sounding from the speakers and quiet, conferring murmuring.

She found the laminated cocktail list hanging from a bit of dirty twine but it took her eyes a moment to focus on the correct cocktail.

'Okay,' Ruth murmured, taking in the ingredients. She straightened and turned back to the girl. 'So, we don't have any orange peel I'm afraid.'

'Just do your best.'

Ruth placed a glass in front of her and arranged the various liquids, all the while aware of the girl's intense gaze. It made her feel self-conscious and clumsy. She forced herself to slow down as she added the sugar and bitters. When it was assembled, she squeezed a cherry onto the lip of the glass.

'No cocktail sticks.' She slid the glass over.

'Thank you.' The girl reached out, running her fingers through the condensation forming on the glass. 'I feel like I should apologise for ordering that.'

Ruth chuckled. 'Don't worry about it. It was fun to make.'

Ruth accepted the twenty-pound note and walked to the till to change it.

The girl had turned on her stool when she returned, watching as another quiz question was read out.

Ruth placed the coins down and nodded towards the people. 'Don't fancy it?'

The girl shook her head. 'I'm not so good at general knowledge.'

'Yeah, me neither. My boss writes the questions. She asks me to help sometimes but I just don't have a clue.'

'I'm sure you have talents in other areas.'

Ruth snorted softly. 'Not sure about that.' She indicated the girl's drink, cradled in one hand. 'How is it?'

'Delicious.' She leaned forward slightly, tightening her grip on her glass. 'Why don't you make yourself one? On me.'

'Are you sure?' The girl nodded. 'Sweet, thank you. That's super nice.' Ruth turned to the bottles of spirits behind her. 'Don't worry. I'm not into all that fancy stuff. I'm pretty cheap.'

The girl chuckled quietly. It was low and dirty and Ruth couldn't help but grin, her back still to the girl. She probably just had one of those naturally seductive voices but Ruth liked to think she was being flirted with.

'Thanks again,' she said, placing her rum and coke down

on the bar.

The girl inclined her head, casting her gaze over the quiz again.

'Are you with someone here?' Ruth questioned, looking over the people and wondering which old, bald-headed man the girl belonged to.

When that got her a raised eyebrow, Ruth smiled and said, 'What?' She nodded at a man sitting hunched over a table, blazer pulled tightly across his broad upper back. 'I know he doesn't look like much, but he's loaded that one, believe me. Proper sugar daddy material. Some girls are into that kind of thing. You definitely wouldn't be the first bored wife or girlfriend sitting at the bar waiting for the quiz to finish.'

'But I'm not bored.' Ria rested her chin demurely on her hand, gracing the room and its occupants with an observant gaze. 'I think,' she said, 'if I had to choose, it would be that one at the front, the one with the long red hair.'

'Fiona?' Ruth raised her eyebrows, watching the girl in question raise her palms, shushing the room in preparation for the next question.

'Although, she's not really my type either.'

Ruth glanced away from her colleague. 'No?'

'No. I prefer girls who are slightly *darker*.'

'Darker?' Ruth smiled. 'Sweet.'

Risarial placed a fingertip on her chest and nodded. 'Inside,' she whispered.

'Hey, Ruthie,' a coarse voice boomed out. 'Can I get me two lagers, ta ducky.'

Dazedly, Ruth pulled her gaze away. 'Yeah, sure,' she said, turning away from Ria. Her hands were shaking she realised. She frowned, grasping the glasses and firmly placing them down on the in front of the man.

'Thanks duck,' he said, glancing sidelong at Ria sitting beside him.

Ruth smiled. *Not your type, mate.*

'You alright there, darling?' the man said, fingers loose

around the two pints. The girl inclined her head at him, eyes falling just short of his. 'What you doing out here tonight then?'

'Enjoying a quiet drink,' she replied, glancing up at Ruth.

From her place leaning back against the shelves, Ruth smiled and folded her arms, enjoying the girl's obvious distaste. The guy—John—she knew was pushy, despite having a wife at home. Pretty gross but common in her line of work unfortunately. She wondered how long it would take before he pushed the girl too far. She seemed like the type to take no shit and Ruth kind of wanted to see it for herself.

'Ah,' John said, leaning over slightly to peer at her drink. 'That's a posh little thing you got there. What's that then, some kind of rum thing?'

'Whiskey.'

'Whiskey? Oh aye. Hope this one here gave you the good stuff. You seem like a lass who's used to the good stuff. Aye, far too pretty for a joint like this.' He planted his two pints back onto the bar, wiped the condensation on his palm down his shirt and leaned in close. 'You can join us if you want. Me and the boys—we got this quiz down. Come pretty up our table and we'll happily split the winnings with you. What do you say, eh? Could help us out with the girly questions.'

When the girl put down her drink on the bar a little too hard, Ruth finally uncrossed her arms and stepped forward. 'Better get that pint to your friend, John. Next round's about to start.'

John looked at her and nodded, an almost chagrined smile on his face, and pulled the two drinks back towards himself. Glancing sidelong at the girl again, he said, 'Thanks again, Ruthie.'

When he was back at his table, the girl sat back and narrowed her eyes at Ruth. 'Thank you, *Ruthie*, for that valiant rescue.'

Ruth waved her away. 'You looked like you were

handling it.' She gestured towards her near-empty glass. 'You want another of your rum things?'

The girl dipped her head. 'I could go for another. If you pour another for yourself, too.'

'Cool.' Ruth turned to prepare the drinks. 'You know, now that you've bought me two drinks, I should probably get your name.'

'Hm, I'm not sure,' the girl teased, tilting her head. A wave of black hair fell over her face, gleaming in the garish overhead bar lights. 'Names are powerful.'

Ruth chuckled. 'Okay. Well, I'll go first then. I'm Ruth. Obviously.'

The girl nodded slightly. Her gaze lowered to the bar as if in thought, then back up to Ruth's. 'Guess it. What do you think my name is?'

Ruth allowed herself to stare under the guise of sizing her up. She stepped back and folded her arms, running her eyes all over the girl's face which was firmly trained on hers. Her gaze zeroed in on a tiny dark freckle at the corner of her mouth, so perfectly placed that Ruth found herself wondering if it had been pencilled on. Then the girl smiled, and that freckle disappeared into the most sensual laughter line Ruth had ever seen. *Fuck*. She swallowed. It should be illegal to be that attractive.

'Talia,' she said on a breath. 'Or something equally as exotic. Can't see you being called something like Becky or Chelsea for some reason.'

The girl watched her for a moment more before saying, 'Ria. I'm Ria.'

'Ria.' Ruth nodded. 'That's nice.' She slid Ria's drink towards her and picked up her own. 'Thanks again for this. My boss hates us accepting drinks but luckily she's not on tonight so we should be good.'

'It would be rude of you not to accept.'

Ruth smiled. 'Wouldn't dream of it.'

It was almost a shock when, forty-five minutes later, the pub erupted into applause and a healthy amount of booing.

Ruth looked over as if coming up from a dream. It'd been forever since she'd got herself lost in conversation like that. She'd almost forgotten she was at work.

The winners—not John's table, Ruth noted—accepted their prizes and people began standing and gathering their belongings.

Ruth straightened up with a sigh. 'Last call. Bear with.'

Just as people began filing towards the bar, Ria recaptured her eyes and asked, 'Ruth, what are your plans for after your shift?'

'Um.' Ruth thought to the cold, uneaten pizza on her dining room table. She'd turned her nose up at it before leaving for work earlier, but she knew she'd get home, fatigued from her shift, and scarf a couple of slices before sitting down and zoning out in front of the telly. Same old.

'Nothing much,' she said.

Ria leant forward, clasping her hands together in a startlingly elegant gesture. 'Would you like to go somewhere with me?' she asked, leaning her head against her clasped hands.

'Go where?'

Ria shrugged. 'Somewhere you can get to know me more. Somewhere where there's dancing, perhaps. I'll let you choose.'

Ruth let her gaze wander over Ria's shoulder as she thought of somewhere they could go. Somewhere gay, for sure. There were half a dozen places in the city that she could choose from but her mind wouldn't cooperate with Ria looking at her like that, a painted red nail tapping restlessly against her cocktail glass.

'Okay,' Ruth eventually said. 'Think I got a place.'

Ria smiled and raised her drink to her lips. 'Wonderful. I'll wait.'

CHAPTER 7

Ruth turned up the collar of her jacket as she led Ria through the dark streets of Manchester. Her breath was visible on the frigid air and the plumes reminded her of the e-cig in her pocket. She pulled it out, took a drag and then extended it to Ria, eyebrow raised.

Ria eyed the thing then shook her head. 'No, thank you.'

'You don't smoke?'

'No.'

Ruth took another pull before pocketing it again. She wound her hands as far as they would go in her jacket, fingers frozen around the cold plastic of the e-cig. 'Definitely in my head but I think it warms me up a bit.'

'This city's dirty enough,' Ria said, kicking a flattened drink can across the pavement. 'No need to fill your lungs even more.'

Ruth pursed her lips. 'Fair enough.'

They continued towards Canal Street; the bar she'd chosen was on one of the side roads just off it. It was Ruth's preferred hangout but as they walked, she found herself reconsidering. Ria seemed so…dignified. Ruth wasn't sure she'd enjoy the small hole-in-wall she usually frequented. They turned down another street and Ruth shrugged inside her jacket. Fuck it. She had never cared what people thought before and she wasn't going to begin now, no matter how attractive she found the girl.

'Just down here,' she murmured, placing her palm on the

small of Ria's back.

The door to the bar, painted a shiny black and always looking like it had just been kicked down, hung open on its hinges and blew lightly in the breeze that was whipping down the street. Ruth reached out and held it still, catching the bassy music from within.

'After you,' she smiled, nodding Ria along. 'I'll go put our coats in the cloakroom if you want.'

Ria nodded and shrugged out of her coat. 'And I will get us a drink.'

Ruth found Ria idling by the bar, two plastic pint cups filled to the brim with red liquid in her hands. The triple vodkas and cherry and raspberry mixers were the only things the place sold unless you fancied a can of god-awful beer.

Ria offered one of them to Ruth as she stepped close, the toes of their shoes almost touching.

'I figured you for a cherry girl,' Ria said.

'That's me.' Ruth accepted the drink. 'Not a flavour thing, more of a moral standing.'

Ria smiled. 'Because raspberries aren't blue?'

Ruth pointed at her, eyes lighting up. 'Exactly. How did you know?'

Ria's eyes slid away from her. 'Heard it before.'

'Well, it's just stupid. Nothing blue about raspberries is there?' Ruth took a sip of her pint. 'Glad someone out there is in the same camp as me.' She looked around. 'Want to get a booth for a bit?'

Ria nodded, gesturing her ahead. Ruth secured them a booth close to the bar. The table and faux leather seat backing were white but with the multi-hued lights above them, they shone red and blue.

Ruth took another sip of her drink before placing it down onto the table. She'd already drank half of it and made a point to slow down. She wasn't nervous exactly, it was more that the girl's presence tonight had been so unexpected, she wasn't sure how to play it. She knew it wouldn't be long before the triple vodkas kicked in and she wouldn't care either way.

Ruth glanced up at Ria, noticing the darkening of her lips as she sipped from her plastic cup. She smiled inwardly. That was another reason why she liked the cherry pints. Whatever food colouring it contained had a way of dyeing your lips and Ruth always thought that was a hot-as-hell look on girls. Like bloodstained. She shuffled forward on the bench, allowing the wave of tipsiness to travel over her, and asked, 'You been here before?'

Ria shook her head slowly before glancing around. It was just filling up at this hour. The patrons were mixed—old weird men who did nothing but nurse a drink and watch everyone else, students who used the place as a cheap watering hole before moving onto the bigger clubs and then a few rocker types who favoured the alternative music they sometimes played here. 'It has an interesting atmosphere.' She looked back at Ruth. 'Suits you somehow.'

Ruth grinned. 'Dark and dingy?'

Under the table, Ria's palm found her knee. 'Just dark.'

'You keep alluding to that,' Ruth said, trying to keep her knee from jiggling. She tilted her head to the side. 'I'm worried I'm giving you the wrong impression.'

'I would disagree,' Ria countered. 'So far you've given me all the right ones.'

Ruth pursed her lips in a pleased smirk and rapped her knuckles lightly on the table in an absent manner. A man swerved into their table on the way to the bar and Ruth followed him with her eyes, mind lost in a foggy haze. She knew Ria was watching her, she could feel it. She kept away from those eyes though; she was trying to make up her mind about things. She wasn't stupid; it was clear what Ria wanted from the night. And it wasn't like she hadn't done the casual sex thing a couple of times before, but even those weren't with complete strangers, more like a friend of a friend she'd met randomly on a night out.

Ruth reached out and pulled her drink to her, eyes finally

meeting Ria's, and suddenly she found she didn't care.

Ria smiled, shaking her plastic cup to show Ruth it was empty. 'Shall we dance now?'

Ruth nodded and stood, legs a tad unsteady. She waved Ria on and weaved after her through the throng on the dance floor and into a dark corner near the speakers. Just as Ria turned back to her, a gust of dry ice blew from somewhere near, swirling around her body so perfectly it was like she'd conjured it. From out of the fog, Ria's hands rose and brushed her shoulders, encouraging her to dance close. When Ruth stepped up to her, hip to hip, Ria's hands fell from her, a teasing glint in her eyes.

Ruth drew in a breath through her nose, resisting the urge to plant her hands on Ria's hips and pull her back. She was thankful they were in a secluded corner, fogged by dry ice. Truth be told, she hadn't danced with someone this dirtily before. She was only glad she'd chosen a gay place, not wanting to think about the heckles they'd be getting from het guys if they were someplace else.

When the music next changed, a number of people on the dance floor cheered. Ruth recognised it as a song used on a popular queer dating show, a song very obviously about sex. It was fast and rhythmic with a low, deep base. All around, people pulled closer to those they were dancing with and Ruth grinned as a guy dressed in heels and a crop-top executed a slut drop before his female friend.

'Like an enchantment,' Ria said into her ear. 'The way they change.'

'Definitely brings the gays to the yard, this song.'

'I like it.'

Ruth smiled, fingers daring to reach out to touch Ria's top. 'Me too.'

The triple vodkas and what she'd had during her shift were definitely coursing their way through her blood now. Her heart was pounding along with the beat and there was a heavy feeling that had taken up residence between her legs. She looked into Ria's eyes and the thought that she'd be having sex with the girl before the night was over was a lot less overwhelming than it had been before. She wanted her, she found—she wanted her badly.

They danced together for a few more songs before Ruth finally had to step away, fanning herself.

'Fuck, I need a drink,' she said, putting a hand to her flushed cheeks. 'If I go to the bar, will you still be here when I get back?'

Ria nodded, stepping backwards to lean against the wall, hands behind her back.

Ruth pointed at her. 'Don't move.'

When she returned with two more cherry pints in hand, Ria was staring at her, her gaze distant and almost sad. It wasn't until Ruth tilted her head in askance that Ria's eyes finally focussed and she smiled, that laughter line deepening her face.

'You alright there?' Ruth handed over the drink.

'I certainly am now.'

Ruth leaned her shoulder against the wall beside her, making sure it brushed up against Ria's. They were of equal height but Ria was slouched slightly, one hand still behind her back, so Ruth was essentially looming over her, shielding her from the rabble on the dance floor. As a rule, Ruth didn't bother with people as tall as herself, or taller. The dynamic made her feel meek, something she hated, but Ria seemed to appeal to that tough side of herself and it made her feel good. And, if she had to admit it, she was a little enraptured with that distant, sad look she saw on her face before. It made her want to kiss her and hold her all at once and in her drunken state, the rush of that was so powerful.

Suddenly wanting to know things about this girl, she asked, 'Are you from here? Manchester?'

Ria shook her head. 'Not originally but I'm staying in an apartment here for the time being.'

'So you're living here then?'

'I am.'

'Sweet. Do you know the city?'

Ria ran a finger around the rim of her plastic cup, gaze low on the swishing red liquid within. 'I'm no stranger to it.'

'Well, I won't offer to play tour guide then,' Ruth teased.

Ria chuckled. 'If it means I get to see you again, offer away.'

Ruth's heart thumped at the inference. 'Alright,' she said. 'We'll figure something out.'

'So,' she began, drawing the word out slightly, 'we essentially had sex on the dance floor earlier and just now agreed to a second date and we haven't even kissed yet.'

Ria smiled at her, her head tilted. She looked charmed and expectant all at once.

Sensing no resistance, Ruth leaned her head forward and put her lips to Ria's. For a moment, Ruth could sense Ria holding her breath before she relaxed back against the wall. Ruth moved with her, coming around to her front and kissing her more firmly, one hand cupped around her face, the other holding her drink between them, careful not to spill any. As the kiss deepened, she moved the cup away so she could step closer, their bodies touching along their lengths.

One of Ria's hands was on her side, hovering there, grazing so lightly.

That heavy feeling between her legs was pulsing now and she found herself calculating how long it would take them to walk back to her flat and if Ria would even say yes if she asked. She was about to put the question to her when Ria suddenly began shimmying her way down her body. Ruth pulled in a breath, glancing at the people paying them no mind on the dance floor, before she realised Ria was only bending down to rid herself of her drink. She smiled knowingly at Ruth as she straightened back up and relieved her of hers too.

Ruth closed her eyes again, this time grasping Ria's waist with both open hands. Ria kissed her back with abandon this time, threading her fingers into Ruth's short hair and scraping her nails against her scalp. Ruth sighed, almost a groan, swaying against Ria as her whole body tingled. She was so sensitive there. Ria scraped with her nails again as if she already knew that and Ruth wondered if she'd discover all her other sweet spots just as quickly. She squeezed Ria's hips, wondering where all hers were too.

When Ruth slipped a thigh between Ria's, Ria pulled back and studied her eyes for a second before gently pushing her away. She said nothing as she took Ruth's hand and pulled her away from the wall.

Ruth let her lead, wondering where they were going as they passed by the cloakroom and exit. Ria stopped outside the accessible toilet. Ruth suppressed a grin. So that's how she wanted to play it. Kinky, but okay.

'That's usually locked,' she told her. 'You need a special type of key.'

Ria glanced at her over her shoulder then turned back to the door. She did something with her hands that Ruth couldn't see and then the door released. Ria threw her a satisfied smile before slipping through it, leaving it open for Ruth to follow.

The toilet's interior was garishly bright. Ruth leant back against the door to close it and after ensuring it was locked, met Ria over at the barest wall.

She had thought Ria had been wearing makeup all night but now, seeing her in the light, it was just that her eyelashes were so dark and long, it gave the illusion that she was. She only hoped her own eyeliner hadn't smudged. It had been a few hours since she'd applied it and she'd sweated plenty on the dance floor. She kissed Ria, so she'd close her eyes and not see either way.

Out of the view of prying eyes, Ria kissed her hard, gladly opening her legs to accept one of Ruth's between them. Ruth let out a small moan at the sensation, now that they were alone. God, this was the hottest thing she'd ever done, with the hottest girl she'd ever hooked up with. She ran her hands up Ria's sides, fingers fanning daringly close to her chest. Just as she put her lips to Ria's neck, Ria span them around so it was her back on the wall.

Ruth's breath stuttered in her chest at the quick movement, especially when Ria began unbuttoning her work shirt. She started from the bottom and when she had bared enough of Ruth's stomach, she got to her knees and pressed her lips to the hot skin there.

Ruth put her hand to the back of Ria's head. She met her own gaze in the mirror opposite as Ria began working on the clasp of her trousers. Shit, this was really happening. The club outside receded to the back of her mind and she closed her eyes, begging silently for what Ria was offering.

It didn't take her long to get what she wanted, and even less time to reach the pinnacle. Her hand flew out to grab a support bar. 'Oh, fuck,' she gasped, pushing the back of her head almost painfully against the tiled wall, hips reaching out for the last of Ria's touch.

When Ria finally rose, her lips were parted, eyes smoky and hard. Not taking her gaze away from Ruth's, she grasped her hand and guided it inside her trousers. Ruth closed her eyes at all the heat she could feel there. Ria removed her own hand, parking her palms either side of Ruth's head.

On a broken breath, she whispered, 'Touch me, Ruth.'

Ruth did. She didn't think anyone outside would hear but she was thankful that Ria was relatively quiet. As she finally reached the point of no return, she lowered her head and bit down hard on the juncture between Ruth's neck and shoulder. Ruth squeezed her eyes against the pain, slowing her hand down when Ria reached down and grasped her wrist.

'*Stop,*' she gasped.

They were quiet as they redid their trousers. Ruth couldn't think of a thing to say. The orgasm had sobered her up big time and she felt tired. As Ria met her gaze, the handle of the door pushed down and they watched it open. A drag queen stood there, her white blonde wig so overly coiffed it almost grazed the top of the door frame.

'*Ew,*' she said, hand on her heart as if she'd had a fright. 'Lesbians.'

Ruth smirked and took Ria's hand, leading them past the drag queen and out of the toilet.

'Shall we go get our coats?' she asked. Ria nodded and they walked to the cloakroom in silence.

CHAPTER 8

Ruth threw her keys towards the tiny table just inside the door. They slipped off, landing with a metallic thunk on the floor but too weary to fish for them, she left them there and tread over to her living room. For a moment she just swayed there, in a haze of fatigue and tired astonishment, replaying the night over in her mind. Then her nose picked up the scent of cold pizza and her mouth watered.

She flipped the cardboard top of it, swallowing down the saliva pooling in her mouth, and freed a slice. It was a veggie pizza, flecked with green peppers and mushrooms which she wasn't too keen on, but she ignored them as she chewed, too hungry to care much.

She slouched down heavily on her sagging sofa, silently thanking Molly for the food. A bit of guilt prickled at her conscience at the thought of her now-ex. She'd only broke up with her barely twenty-four hours ago and she'd already slept with someone else. Pretty shitty of her. Involuntarily, her mouth quirked into a smile. But fuck, not like she was going to pass up an opportunity like tonight.

Despite her tiredness, the place between her legs tingled as she thought of their toilet encounter. She hoped they'd get to do that again. Her gaze flicked to her bedroom. Maybe in a bed this time. She'd had half a mind to invite Ria back to her place afterwards but then she remembered the stale garlic permeating the air and all the clothes piling up on the floor waiting for her next day off to be washed, and decided she just couldn't. Ria hadn't invited her back to hers either. Still, she had Ria's number tucked up safe in her phone now so she didn't feel too bad about how the night had ended, especially after the goodbye kiss they'd shared beside the canal.

Chucking the crust of her pizza slice back into the box, Ruth picked up another. Though her flat was silent at this hour of the morning, something that usually discomforted her, her mind was so active with flashbacks she didn't once reach out to flick on the telly.

∞ ∞

Risarial turned to the side at the last minute, throwing up the contents of her stomach into a fake potted plant on the side of the rooftop terrace. The vomit was pink, a nod to whatever cherry-flavoured poison she'd drank tonight. She raised a trembling hand and wiped her mouth with the side of it. *Oh, Ruth.* She chuckled wryly. *Only for you.*

She placed her hands down on the cold rail, looking out over the dark, nearly quiet city. It was never truly silent here. The human world rarely was. They scurried like mice, leaving traces of themselves around like droppings.

A wind whipped at her hair and she tilted her head back, welcoming the frigid hit of air. Though her stomach quivered with sickness, the rest of her body thrummed for different reasons. She hadn't meant it to go that far, she really hadn't, but one touch of Ruth's lips on hers had brought with it an onslaught of memories and sensations. She'd let herself slide into the past, pretending that she and Ruth were an item again and they were just on another of their after dark adventures. Risarial smiled. There had been many of those. Ruth always seemed most herself in the shadows of nightfall, less guarded and more free. Wild.

Risarial gripped the rail tightly, her jaw set. She was impatient to get them back to that point. She hated having to play this oh so slow game. Ruth knew her, dammit. Well, as well as she could. A wave of fury washed over her, but it wasn't aimed at Ruth, or at herself. It was directed at the thing that had destroyed their union in the first place. Risarial dragged her eyes over the city's skyline, wondering if they were still here, concealed somewhere like the vermin they were.

Slowly her grip released, and she drew in a steadying breath. She turned to go inside, the queen-sized bed in the penthouse beckoning her. She needed the rest; she had another day of scheming ahead of her.

CHAPTER 9

Ruth groaned as she read the text from Sheila. She wanted her to take over Molly's shift which started in an hour. Guess she jacked in her job after all. *Shit.* Ruth groaned again. It was her day off for fuck's sake, and she was knackered from the night before. She blew out a raspberry before pulling herself out of bed. She rattled off an affirmative text to Sheila and picked up her collection of dirty mugs from her bedside table, intent on brewing herself the strongest coffee she could.

At least there wouldn't be any people around to bother her, bar the guys who dropped off the kegs in the mornings, and it was Sheila who usually dealt with them. Ruth leant against the countertop as the kettle boiled, tapping a finger restlessly against her crossed arms. She wondered if Sheila would be mad with her. She seemed pretty blunt in her text but then she wasn't the fuzziest at the best of times. Technically it *was* her fault Molly had quit. She wondered what she'd said to Sheila about that. Ruth sighed, hefting the kettle just before it clicked off and pouring it on top of a healthy serving of coffee grounds. Guess she'd soon find out.

❧ ❧

Ruth glanced at the clock behind the bar. She'd been at this for almost two hours now and still had the ladies toilets upstairs to clean. She picked up her bucket and with mop in

51

hand, started up the stairs. She didn't know how Molly got through her shifts so quickly. She always had at least half an hour to spare and they'd usually spent that kissing in the cellar. Ruth wondered now if she'd ever see the girl again.

Ruth let the old, heavy wooden door to the toilets swing shut behind her and blew out a breath between pursed lips. She was exhausted and overheated from hauling the outside furniture and furiously scrubbing the brass drip trays.

She dropped her bottles of cleaning fluids to the carpet and leaned back against the sink countertops, head on one shoulder. She was in a funk and didn't know why. Autumn sun shone in through the window, piercing her eyes where the frosted film peeled from one corner. A huge dead spider lay in a crumpled heap on the windowsill. Ruth picked it up with her yellow-gloved fingers and dropped it into the bin.

She turned to the two toilet cubicles and tipped her head back with a groan. *Fuck this.* It had been years since she'd had to do this and she couldn't say she missed it.

Releasing a breath, she kicked open the first cubicle.

҂ ҂

Sheila was behind the bar when she finally came back downstairs.

'You almost done?' she asked, throwing her a quick glance. She had a tray of change in her hands, stabbing at the temperamental till until it released.

'I'm done.' Ruth opened the door to the cellar, holding it ajar with her bum so she could pull the mop through.

'Good. Me too. Meet me upstairs when you've dropped all that off.'

҂ ҂

Ruth went straight to Sheila's kitchen and poured herself a glass of water before plonking herself on the small sofa.

'Thanks for that, pet,' Sheila said, lighting up a cigarette.

The skin on her thumb was worn away from flicking a lighter so often.

Ruth snorted. 'Don't mention it.'

'So.' Sheila leaned back, armchair creaking loudly. 'What did you do to the poor girl, eh?'

Ruth frowned. 'You mean Molly? Why is it something I've done?'

'Well, it wasn't you crying into the head of a mop yesterday morning, was it?'

Ruth sighed, glancing away. 'I just wasn't feeling it anymore. Not a crime, is it?'

Sheila tutted. 'She was a nice girl. Thought you were into it.'

'I was…' Ruth sounded unconvinced even to herself. It still wasn't something she could rightly explain.

'Hope you're not doing that thing again.'

'What thing?'

'You know'—Sheila raised her cigarette-wielding hand and waved it at her—'that self-sabotage, *I-can't-deal-with-a-happy-relationship* thing.'

Ruth frowned even deeper. 'What?' She didn't know what that meant.

Sheila sighed. 'Never mind. Your life. But now I need a new bloody cleaner. Any ideas?'

Ruth pursed her lips and shook her head. Most of the friends she had, she'd met working at the pub. Unwittingly, her mind wandered to Ria and she must have been smiling because Sheila suddenly barked, 'What?'

Ruth looked at her. 'I met someone last night.'

Sheila breathed out a huff. 'That didn't take long.'

'I met her here, at the quiz night.'

Sheila's brows knitted. 'God's sake Ruth, my pub isn't your own personal dating pool.'

Ruth chuckled. 'Her name's Ria.'

'Right.'

'And she's gorgeous. Like fucking *gorgeous*.'

'Uh-huh.'

53

'We went out afterwards.' Ruth smiled wider. 'We had sex in the club loos.'

Sheila raised her eyebrows. 'Dirty girl.' Ruth laughed. 'So?' Sheila pressed. 'How was your little toilet tryst?'

'Really good actually,' Ruth said, nodding. 'Really bloody good. It felt like proper grownup sex.'

Sheila let out a surprised cackle, smoke blowing from her lips in a whoosh. 'It felt like what? Grownup sex, eh.'

'Yeah, like it really flowed. That's never really happened before.'

'Grownups do it in bed, darl. You might want to try that next time.' Sheila regarded her shrewdly. 'Reckon there'll be a next time?'

'Definitely.' Ruth nodded. 'For sure.' Then she held up a hand. 'Just sex, though. Casual.' Shaking her head, she said, 'Fuck another relationship right now.'

'Mm.' Sheila nodded slowly, unconvinced. 'You still doing your smoothies and all that?'

Ruth shrugged. 'Sometimes.' When Sheila gave her a look, she said, 'It's not been too bad, my head.'

'Take your word for it. Just be careful.' She gestured towards her box of ciggies beside her. 'Want one?'

Ruth waved her off. 'Given up, haven't I?'

'Please. You've just swapped your poison for another.'

'Yeah well, at least my shit tastes good. Kill me slower, too.' Ruth stood up. 'Anyway, I'm gonna go. It's my day off, you know.'

Sheila stubbed out her cigarette. 'Alright, chickie. Make the most of it. You're on the open tomorrow.'

'Yeah, don't remind me.'

After giving a last chin scratch to Bella, Ruth shrugged on her jacket and left the pub. She still felt wiped so she found the nearest café, ordered herself a black coffee and took it back to her flat. The place still smelled of stale pizza, her laundry was all over the floor and Ria still hadn't text her. Maybe she was waiting for Ruth to? She sat down at her dining table, tapping a blunt nail on the cold, black screen of her phone.

It was still morning. She would hate to seem too keen. She leant her chin on a palm, glancing up at the large clock opposite her, ticking loudly in the silent room. The glass face had a large crack in it, snaking up like a spider web, obscuring the number seven. Last time Sheila had visited, she'd promised to buy Ruth a replacement. She never had but Ruth didn't mind the cracks too much. The ticking though, sometimes that grated on her. At times, like now, the ticking was so stark, it sounded like it came from inside her head. She should get up, put on some music or something but she remained sitting, stiffening up in her jacket, the tips of her fingers now as cold as her blank phone screen.

When sirens flared past her flat, drowning out the ticking, Ruth took in a breath and stood up.

'Do your fucking washing,' she whispered, bending down to yank a crumpled hoodie from the floor.

A few minutes later, the washing machine was whirling, soap sudding up the glass door, and Ruth sat on the floor beside it, staring through the blinds of the window in front of her. Her phone sat on the table, forgotten.

At work, she always craved her day off, counting down the days, the hours. But when it came, it was always kind of flat. The lack of people, the lack of anything to fill up her mind, left room for other, darker, things to snake their way in. Ruth let her head fall back against the cabinet behind her and sighed.

God, it had been a while since she'd felt like this. She'd almost forgotten. Hoped it had gone away, maybe. With Molly, it hadn't been so bad. It was nice, having her around, always dragging Ruth here and there, making her do stuff. Ruth bit her bottom lip. Maybe it had been dumb to end things. But then again, that in itself was probably a shit reason to stay with someone, wasn't it?

With difficulty, Ruth got to her feet. She couldn't sit around like this all day, she just couldn't. Remembering

Sheila's earlier comments, she grasped her blender and pulled it towards her on the countertop. It was probably a placebo, the smoothie thing, but Ruth still felt it helped a bit. When things had first got bad about a year ago, she'd tried meds, but they fucked her up too badly. She'd had to have two weeks off work when they upped her dose and she never, ever wanted to feel like that again. So she'd taken Sheila's advice to try some herbal stuff instead. St John's wort, ginseng, some other stuff—all blended up with some banana and frozen berries. Tasted good and didn't mess with her chemistry. Not in a bad way anyway.

Smoothie in hand, Ruth flicked on her speakers, turning up the music until she couldn't hear the ticking of the clock anymore. She'd finally throw out the pizza box today and maybe dust the place. She just had to get to six o'clock—that's when the good telly came on, then she could sleep, and then, finally, she'd be back at work.

CHAPTER 10

Risarial had left her phone at the apartment. Despite that, she still felt her hands slipping into the depths of her coat pocket, seeking it out. It irked just how much she yearned to contact Ruth—to see her again. Walking along the grey, cold streets of Manchester, she shook her hair out viciously. Patience had never been her game. It stretched the limits of herself, quashed her into something which sorely went against her nature.

Worth it. She's worth it.

Biting her inner lip hard, she stepped into the camera dealer. It was a pokey shop, heavily shelved, stocked with most every camera to grace human history. Ignoring the old man at the till, Risarial craned her head upwards. The cameras along the top shelf were devices Risarial could only wonder at—huge, boxy contraptions that looked more like the accordions from her world—whilst those at eye-height were recently refurbished and—hopefully—working cameras.

Risarial reached out and plucked a camera. She turned to the shop owner.

'This. How much for it?'

He pointed. 'Says right there, ducky. Sixty quid.'

Risarial nodded, plopping it down onto the counter. She dug into her pocket, brought out a few notes and tossed them next to the camera. As the man rang up her order, he rattled on about the camera's care, so earnestly that Risarial fought the urge to roll her eyes. She listened idly, eyes wandering over to the glass door. It was raining again. She took her wears quickly and walked out into it.

The mizzle felt like home. She licked the drops from her lips. They tasted sour—just like the tap water here, just like the food. Chemical-laden and astringent but she liked it somehow. It tasted like the first time she'd tasted Ruth, the heat of her mouth and the sweat from her pores. Risarial looked down at the rain-dotted pavement and gripped her bags tighter, knowing her eyes were glowing orange and being unable to stop them. Heavens, she had to see her again soon.

At the apartment, Risarial placed down her bags, the smell of fresh fish drifting up from one of them. She crossed to the fridge and placed the fillets inside, along with vegetables and a strange sauce she'd tried the last time she was here. At least she hoped it was the same stuff. It was oily and yellow, with mustard seeds bobbing at the bottom of the glass bottle. It cost almost as much as the fish, fish she wasn't entirely sure she wanted anymore.

When she'd arrived at the seafood market, there had been somewhat of a commotion. The owner was standing at the freezer, holding the doors of it open and showing a couple of customers something inside.

Annoyed at having to wait, Risarial craned her head to see what the holdup was. That was when she'd caught sight of the dead nixie, laying slackly over a crude bed of ice. The thing must have glamoured itself before it died. To those gawping, it looked like some sort of monkfish, only more bloated with thin tendrils flowing from its spine—the nixie's hair.

The glamour wouldn't last. When the customers finally moved on and the owner wandered over to her, Risarial subtly twisted her hand and the freezer slammed shut, echoing like a gunshot through the market. The owner jumped and made to turn back but Risarial bade him forwards. When he'd next open the freezer, the nixie would be gone.

Risarial was still wondering on its death when the sound of muffled sobbing reached her ears. She sighed and made for the dressing room. The man had his eyes closed but his head roved like a newborn's, incoherently searching for his mother. Tears streaked his ashy face. He was resisting her glamour quicker than he had the last time she'd stayed here. If it wasn't for the fact he kept soiling his trousers, she'd almost be impressed. Risarial stalked over to him and knelt.

'Stop throwing off your shackles,' she said, running a hand down the man's face to quieten him.

That dealt with, she returned to her shopping and brought out the camera, turning in circles as she thought of where to put it. The kitchen island would do. It faced the front door. Ruth was bound not to miss it there. She placed it down on the corner, tweaking it until it sat just so, then paced backwards until she was at the front door. *Perfect.*

Only then did she feel ready to pick up her phone and unearth Ruth's number.

Ruth felt her phone buzz in her pocket but it was just past noon and there was a lunch rush on at the pub. She didn't get her break until after three and even then she only had enough time to scarf down a pasta mix from the shop and take a few hasty pulls from her e-cig. She didn't check her phone. It would either be her phone company or the girl from two nights ago. Anybody else would message her on an app.

A part of her did want to check if Ria had texted, but she was still fighting the monsters from the day before. It didn't help that she'd bumped into Molly on the way to work and the girl had all but blanched at seeing her. It kind of hammered home that the last thing she needed right now was to be getting involved with somebody else. No matter how casual she'd told Sheila it would be, and no matter how attractive the somebody was.

After the lunch rush, things calmed down to an almost unusual amount. No longer needing to focus to keep up with orders, she let her mind drift, trying to rekindle the magic from that night. She looked to the stool Ria sat on, unoccupied now, and conjured up her face smirking back at her from under a fall of dark hair.

'What are you staring at?' Sheila said, brushing past her and breaking her thoughts.

'Nothing.'

'This place is supposed to be haunted, you know.'

Back turned, Ruth rolled her eyes. 'I know. You've said. Millions of times.'

'One of the oldest pubs in the city,' Sheila went on. 'Not many can say that.'

'I'm sure not many care.'

Sheila paused in her pouring of a drink. 'What's got your knickers in a twist today then? That girl ghosted you or something? Might not be too late to fix things with Molly. Still no luck on a cleaner.'

Ruth took money from a customer and watched them walk away with their drink before replying, 'She hasn't ghosted. I haven't messaged her yet.'

'So what's up then?'

'Dunno. Just feeling a bit down today.' She shrugged. 'Been a while. Guess I was due an attack of the morbs.'

'The whats?'

'The *morbs*.' Ruth smiled. 'It's a Victorian saying. Read it on Google once. Means, you know, the sads. And yes, before you ask, I've been doing the smoothies. Need to pick up some more fruit after work.'

'Glad to hear it.' Sheila glanced up, surveying the pub. 'I'll let you go a bit earlier today if this quiet keeps up. Maybe you can message that girl then, eh?'

Ruth frowned slightly. 'Molly or Ria?'

'Either.' Sheila patted her on the back. 'Whichever will cheer you up.'

Ruth watched Sheila walk away and then, seeing no one needing her immediate attention, pulled out her phone behind the cover of a pillar. The text was from Ria. A prickle of interest ran through her at reading the words, *Want to redeem that second date tomorrow evening?*

CHAPTER 11

Ruth stood in the small green, looking up at the apartment building. It was lit up in the dusky evening, a patchwork of incandescent and warm, buttery light. Ruth could see Halloween stickers tacked to some of the windows. She texted Ria to say that she'd arrived, for some reason reluctant to use the intercom, and stepped up to the front door. Her black, faux leather leggings creaked as she shifted from foot to foot in the cold, hands deep in the pockets of her padded denim jacket.

Ria didn't respond to her text but soon she was in front of Ruth on the other side of the door, lips tugged up in a coy grin.

'Hello,' she said when she opened it, leaning forward to brush her cheek with her lips.

Ruth smiled back. 'Hey. You look nice.'

Ria smiled wider. 'As do you.'

They took the lift in silence. Ruth's nerves had been too jangled to take in the sight of Ria properly when she met her at the door but she took her in now, capturing her reflection in the mirror. Shit. The attractiveness hit her all over again. It wasn't as visceral as the first time they'd met but Ria's magnetism was like nothing Ruth had ever felt in a girl before. It almost made her want to…rub up against her or something equally as weird.

They stepped out of the lift and Ruth lifted her nose to the savoury scents that suddenly filled the corridor. 'God, I hope that's coming from your flat,' she murmured.

'You are in luck,' Ria murmured back, pushing open the flat door.

Ruth followed her inside, humming at the smells wafting from the oven. 'Smells amazing.'

Then she looked around at the large, open-planned apartment and issued a low whistle. 'Fancy.' She was mesmerised by the LED waterfall sitting beside the telly. It was slowly fading in and out of a myriad of colours. 'Do you have this place to yourself?'

'Yes.' Ria knelt down by the oven and opened it, moving her face out of the way of the eruption of steam. 'We'll eat and then I'll show you around.'

Ruth nodded and pulled out one of the seats. 'Sounds good to me. I'm starving.'

There were two glasses on the table already filled with red wine. Ria gently lowered the casserole dish onto the table and with a metal spoon, lifted the fillets onto the plates beside the side salad and herbed potatoes.

'This looks incredible,' Ruth said, eyeing the food greedily. She was a sucker for well-cooked fish.

Ria returned the casserole dish to the countertop before sitting herself at the table. She picked up her wine glass and gently clinked it with Ruth's. 'Here's to seeing each other again.'

Ruth drank a hearty mouthful, enjoying the subtle burn of it. She hoped it would do its thing quickly. She was feeling a little out of sorts. It was different from the other night when they'd met at the pub. It was an open space, filled with people and she had a task then—to make drinks and see that Ria was comfortable. Now it was just the two of them, sitting opposite each other without even the soothing of background music. It would be intense in any situation but Ria was particularly, well, starey was the only word that came to mind. She kind of reminded Ruth of a predator. Yeah, that was it. Ruth subtly tapped her fingers on the table at the rightness of her discovery.

Well, she was a predator who could cook at least. It didn't take Ruth long to clear her plate. She almost mourned her last mouthful. She sat back with her wine and waited for Ria to finish. Something touched her leg, stroking up the length of her calf and back down.

'Been a long time since I've played footsie with someone,' Ruth smiled, nudging her back with her foot.

Ria eyed her over her fork, cat-like and sly. Finally, she placed down her cutlery.

'So,' Ruth began. 'How come you wanted to see me again?'

One of Ria's eyebrows rose ever so slightly. 'Did we not have a good time the other night?' she asked. 'Perhaps even one you want to repeat?'

Ruth nodded. 'Yeah, 'course. I had a great night. It's just…Look.' Ruth sighed. 'I'm going to be totally honest with you here. I just got out of a relationship.' Ria's leg paused in its stroking. 'And I'm not sure me getting involved with someone else so soon is a good idea. There's more reasons than that but that's just the main one. I still wouldn't mind hanging out but I don't have much to give anyone right now. Just…don't want to lead you on or anything.'

Ruth picked up her glass and drained it, watching as Ria pursed her lips, nodding slowly. 'That's…noble.'

Ruth raised a palm. 'Sorry.'

'No. Don't be. I appreciate your honesty.' She smiled slightly. 'And I'd still be interested in hanging out.'

Ruth smiled. 'Sweet.' She gestured to her cleared plate. 'This was great, by the way. You're an ace cook.'

Fluidly, Ria rose and picked up their plates. 'Thank you,' she said, back turned. She opened the dishwasher then seemed to freeze, hovering there.

'Alright there?' Ruth asked.

Ria turned back towards her slightly. 'This new apartment…I'm not sure how it works.'

Ruth pushed out her chair and stood up. 'Let's have a look.' She came to Ria's side. 'It's only fair I do this anyway, since you cooked for us.'

Gently, she put her hands on Ria's hips and guided her out of the way. Ria leaned against the kitchen counter, arms crossed as she watched. As Ruth set up the wash sequence, she became aware of Ria's gaze, feeling that same prickly feeling she had the first night they'd met, when Ria had watched her make up her cocktail. It was disconcerting and pleasant all at once and Ruth felt a tickling warmth settle between her legs.

'There,' she whispered, turning back to Ria. She nodded to somewhere behind her. 'Want to show me the rest of this place?'

There wasn't really much to show her apart from the bathroom so Ria took her straight to the bedroom, as Ruth hoped she would.

'So this is where the magic happens?' she quipped, eyeing the ridiculously large bed in the centre of the room.

Ria sidled up behind her, hands falling onto her hips as she replied in a whisper, 'This is where it's going to happen.'

Ruth smiled and turned. There were only the headboard lights on in here, the glow of them dim and warm. The shadowed room buoyed her. She placed her lips to Ria's neck, kissing gently as the last nerves of the evening fled.

'Go get on the bed,' she said, sliding off her jacket.

Ria did as bade, though she eyed Ruth in a way that told her the tables probably wouldn't stay turned this way. She rarely took the submissive role in bed. Pretending to be the one in control usually made her feel like she was but she got the impression that when Ria took the lead, it wasn't because she was pretending.

Ruth crawled onto the bed, pausing as it undulated beneath her. 'Water bed?' she asked, gaze flicking up to Ria's. One of Ria's shoulders lifted in a shrug. 'Bouncy.'

Ria reached out and aided her the rest of the way, stroking open palms over Ruth's back and pulling them flush together. Her legs enveloped Ruth and Ruth pushed into her, kissing her soundly on the lips. She felt Ria fall slack beneath her and smiled at the surrender.

When they'd both divested each other of their clothing and one of Ruth's hands was somewhere between Ria's legs, Ria reached out and touched her cheek with two of her fingers. Her mouth was slightly parted, dark eyes hooded and there was a pink flush rising on her chest.

'Ruth,' she whispered, a soft gust of breath against Ruth's lips. Ruth looked at her questioningly, her hand slowing almost to a stop, but Ria shook her head once, clamping her thighs around Ruth's hand. 'Don't stop it. Don't stop.'

Ruth broke her gaze and redoubled the effort of her hand until Ria's head flew back and she gasped out her pleasure loudly.

Afterwards, Ruth moved back onto her knees, gazing at Ria. There was something in those eyes, something she couldn't quite decipher. She wasn't sure she like it.

'Come up behind me,' she said.

Slowly, Ria sat up and situated herself behind Ruth, arms immediately reaching round to touch her. She closed her eyes and sighed, shutting herself off from the heaviness of Ria's intensity. It felt good then, more anonymous, and she let herself enjoy the deftness of Ria's fingers, fingers which didn't hesitate in knowing how to touch her.

It didn't take much convincing after that for her to stay the night. Ria woke her up twice to continue what they'd started the night before and by the second time, her body was so exhausted that she could only give back.

The blinds on Ria's windows were complete blackouts and she was shocked to see it was past ten in the morning when she finally woke up.

There was a tickling sensation on her back which she identified as Ria's fingers, swimming up and down her spine. As she lay there, a palm replaced the fingers, cupping around her shoulder blade, one thumb stroking the mandala tattoo there. It was nice but felt kind of propriety and her reservations from the night before came rushing back.

Drawing in a breath, Ruth finally turned. 'Hey,' she said.

At seeing her awake, Ria smiled. 'Good morning.'

Ruth didn't know what to say after that. She should probably leave. She had work later and a few chores to get done beforehand. She was about to excuse herself when Ria asked, 'Breakfast?'

Ruth ran a hand over her face, yawning. 'Sure,' she replied, nodding. 'I'm pretty hungry.' She glanced at Ria. 'You know, after last night.'

Ria's smile deepened into a smirk and she reached over to kiss Ruth on the cheek before leaving the bed. She crossed over to the blinds and raised them. The morning light hit Ria's naked body and Ruth enjoyed the way her eyes squinted at the assault. Okay, she was looking kind of cute right there. Cute and sexy as hell.

'Is there anyone down there?' Ruth asked. Ria was still looking out of the window, her spine straight, chest rising and falling steadily, like a queen surveying her kingdom.

'No one who would dare to look up.'

Ruth chuckled. 'I would. If I was down there.'

Ria finally turned back to her. 'No need to be so far away to look.'

Ruth left the bed, turning back to fix the duvet and pillows out of politeness. In the kitchen, Ria was standing at the fridge, clad in a man's shirt which only reached her thighs.

'That's a good look,' Ruth said, coming to sit on an island stool. She glanced to her left, capturing the camera sitting beside her. She'd noticed it last night but had been a little preoccupied to say anything. 'Hey, does this thing work?'

Ria glanced up. 'Yes. I hope so.'

Ruth pulled the camera over. 'Are you a photographer?'

Ria freed a pot of sliced fruit from the fridge, setting it beside a carton of butter. 'New hobby,' she said.

'I love photography.' Ruth turned the camera over in hands. 'It's kind of my thing. I urbex—you know, urban exploring. Take photos of abandoned places.'

From a bread bin, Ria pulled out a wrapped bloomer loaf. 'Oh, really?' She began slicing the loaf with an enormous bread knife. 'That sounds…entertaining.'

Ruth chuckled. 'You don't sound all that eager. It's cool, I know it's not everyone's cup of tea.'

'It's just not something I've tried. Perhaps…'

'Perhaps what?'

'Perhaps you could show me.' She pointed at the camera with the knife. 'I've yet to use that thing. I'm not the best with technology. Your expertise will most likely be of use.'

Ruth smiled, the fatigue of a night with little sleep erasing itself in an instant. 'Yeah? We could do that, definitely.'

Ria smiled back, sliding towards her a plate of buttered bread and fruit slices.

Ruth picked at the bread idly as her mind raced through her schedule. 'Well, I'm working today, tomorrow as well. How about Thursday? Are you free then?'

'I'll make it so.'

CHAPTER 12

Risarial tapped her foot impatiently, watching her youngest sister squatting in front of her prisoner. She was dressed in a pair of the man's huge leather shoes and a fur coat she'd unearthed from heaven-knows-where.

'Pretty human,' she murmured, stroking along his jawline. 'Almost fae in bone.'

'Put him down, Earlie. He's been badly behaved this week.'

Earlie pouted. 'Have you?' She captured a tear from his cheek on a fingertip and put it in her mouth. She grimaced. 'Tastes of despair.' She turned to Risarial. 'I don't think he likes you.'

'Out,' Risarial repeated, pointing to the door.

Tripping in the oversized shoes, Earlie did as instructed.

On the balcony, Cerulean stood with her forearms on the rail, the night's breeze ruffling the curls at her neck. She'd parked herself there as soon as she'd arrived and Risarial had yet to displace her.

'You get used to it eventually,' Risarial said, reaching out for the bottle of wine resting on the tiny balcony table. It was fairy wine, a gift from her sisters: a light pink liquid encased in an hourglass-shaped bottle. Where her fingers grasped it, the glass glowed blue.

'All those lights,' Cerulean said, shaking her head. 'And it *stinks*.'

Risarial smirked. 'Now that, you never get used to.'

'They're not fae?' Cerulean's eyes flitted between all the tiny flickering lights.

Risarial stepped up beside her. 'No.' She pointed. 'Those red ones are cars. Their vehicles. And all those over there are from their houses.'

'And those colourful ones?' Cerulean asked Ria, nodding towards a light fading in and out in the distance.

'I don't know. Perhaps a fountain. Perhaps something else.'

Behind them, Earlie issued a soft sigh. 'They remind me of my mortal.'

'She's not yours anymore,' Risarial reminded her.

'This is her city now. This is her Manchester.'

Risarial looked over her shoulder. 'Don't even think about it.'

Earlie only smiled, her eyes faraway, pale irises catching the glow of the city lights.

'And how is *your* mortal?' Cerulean asked, at last wrenching her gaze away from the view to regard her oldest sister. 'Were you well received?'

Risarial stared into the night, recalling her and Ruth's less than loving reunion and her hasty decision to rid Ruth of her memories of her. Her chest still pinched at what she had done.

'Ruth was…displeased to see me again.' The words tasted sour. Her jaw tightened and she fought down a wave of anger; she wasn't even sure what the fury was directed at.

'What happened?' Earlie asked, eyes wide and earnest.

'I gave us a second chance. A chance to do it right.'

Cerulean regarded her shrewdly and Risarial held still, giving her time to figure it out. 'You took away her memories.'

Risarial nodded once.

Earlie issued a quiet gasp. 'You began again.'

'You carry the feelings for the both of you,' Cerulean mused. 'Hoping she will catch up.'

'She will.' Risarial's voice was firm.

'Will you tell us about the first time?' Earlie asked. 'Tell us how you came to love her.'

'And what went wrong,' Cerulean added.

Normally Risarial would bark at them to leave but the wine had loosened her mind, no doubt exactly what Cerulean had intended.

'We met in the summer,' Risarial answered. 'At a…at a revel. For humans. It was hot and oh so dry.' She recalled how breezes had whipped the sandy ground into eddies and how the humans had crowded the drinking fountains like horses at a trough. 'This revel, it was not like anything from home. They have huge machines which throw out music, so loud the ground shakes and you think your heart might stop.' Risarial smiled. 'The humans had been eating tiny little pills all day and by dusk you would think they were glamoured. So happy, so malleable. And the sky was so red that night.' She closed her eyes. 'I looked away from the sun and saw Ruth.'

'And you were in love?' Earlie whispered.

Risarial sighed. 'Not so simple, Earlie. Not all humans are like yours. Ruth…she's different. She's independent, distrustful of almost everyone and sometimes as mean as any kelpie. She merely enraptured me at first.'

'And it matured into love,' Cerulean finished for her. More softly, she asked, 'And how did it end?'

'A scourge from our world,' Risarial all but growled.

'Ours?'

'A redcap, tossed above the hill for heaven-knows-what.'

'An exiled fae?'

Risarial nodded. 'She wanted to go home. She wanted me to petition Father. I told her no. She grew angered and from her anger, struck a deal.' Risarial drew in a silent breath. 'A kiss and she wouldn't kill Ruth.'

'A kiss?' Earlie whispered.

Risarial's fingers gripped her wine glass. 'She wanted to taste home.'

Slowly, Cerulean said, 'And your mortal saw.'

Risarial chuckled darkly. 'If I thought redcaps were easily angered…Ruth, she cursed me. Wished me dead. Wished herself dead. Banished me back beneath the hill. She loves like the fae,' Risarial ended on a breath.

'You could have explained,' Cerulean reasoned.

Risarial shook her head. 'Some mortals can withstand the truth. Most cannot. There are cracks in Ruth's mind, more so than most. I fear the truth would shatter her.'

An unwelcome burning started behind her eyes and Risarial nearly started when Earlie's hand touched her, curling gently around her wrist. 'I wish upon all that you get your mortal to love you again, sister.'

Risarial smiled slightly. 'As do I, Earlie.'

CHAPTER 13

Ruth sat on the no access gate, swinging her booted legs and hoping Ria would find her okay. She probably should have offered to get the bus with her from the city but she wanted to relish the ride over and savour some of the solitude first. That was what drew her to urbexing in the first place. She liked to be alone in lonely places.

She scuffed her toe over the dirty concrete, poised on the border between the industrial state and the forest. The tiny chapel she wanted to take Ria to was about a mile at her back. According to the forum there wasn't much left of it but it was easy to get in to and was somewhere that wasn't too dangerous or illegal.

Ria found her just as she was clearing space on her camera's memory card. She dropped the camera to rest on its strap against her stomach and got to her feet.

'Hey. You ready?' she asked. In answer, Ria raised her own camera. 'Did you put film in it like I told you?' Ruth reached out and took it from her. 'Here. Let me just check.'

Fiddling with Ria's camera, she led her around the gate and onto the barely-there forest path. Satisfied, she gave the camera back, taking in Ria's tight black-on-black outfit as she did. She looked away just as quickly. She found it strange how reluctant she was to look at Ria sometimes. It wasn't shyness or anything close, just a strange resistance she had no choice but to abide. Probably something to do with her unwillingness to get attached to anyone new right now.

'Where does this wicked forest lead to?' asked Ria.

'An abandoned chapel.' Ruth reached out to brush a branch away from her face. 'Dates back to the 12th century. Well, the site does anyway. Not sure about the chapel itself. Might have been built a bunch of times over.'

'And that's old?'

Ruth chuckled. 'Yeah, that's pretty old.'

The chapel sat in a clearing of both grass and stone. They came upon it just as the sun broke the cloud for the first time that day and doused everything in a bright autumn yellow.

'It is tiny,' Ruth mused, eyeing the faded, grey stone building, fingers already on the buttons of her camera.

The door to it was barred so they walked around to a window devoid of any glass and stepped through. The chapel would be in complete shadow if not for the sun shining through the stained glass high on the northernmost wall, bleeding colour onto the dark wood of the pews.

'There's a lot more of it than I thought there would be,' Ruth said, taking in the small number of pews and intact altar. 'Pretty cool. Need to take some pics before this light goes.'

Ria looked around too, her face a still mask of such concentration and interest it made Ruth pleased to see.

'What was the purpose of this structure?' she asked, running a fingertip through the dirt on top of a water font.

'Um, it's a chapel,' Ruth said, brows knitting. 'You know, like a church. So people would have prayed here and stuff.' Ruth smirked over at her. 'You never been in a church before? Are you the devil or something?'

Angling her camera to the shadowed ceiling, Ria pursed her lips. 'I've been called similar and equal.'

Ruth touched the ends of the pews as she navigated back down the aisle, slowly trailing after Ria. 'Why? By who?'

Ria turned to her just as the sun was swallowed back behind cloud, rendering her face unreadable. Unreadable yet...Ruth stared—it was there again, that something, that message she just couldn't get. Always there. Here in the middle of the forest though, Ruth felt more of a thrill than the usual discomfort.

'I think…if I was here when these ghosts were,' Ria ran a hand over an imp carved into the pillar, 'I'd be forbidden to set foot in such a place as this.'

'Well yeah, you fuck girls,' Ruth answered. She wasn't sure that was what Ria was implying but her statement was too vague and weird that Ruth needed the levity. That thrill struck her again at just how little she knew about this girl. 'Me neither, on that count.'

'Sinning is better in company.' Ria smiled at her and Ruth somehow knew she was doing that binding thing, trying to get under her skin, striving for connection. She let her off this time. Everything was less intense when they were hiding behind their cameras, pointing away from the other.

Ruth walked to the other side of the chapel, putting a pillar between her and Ria. On the ground, greenery was starting to sprout up and Ruth reckoned it wouldn't be long until the wood in the church gave way to rot and melted back into the forest it probably came from in the first place. She was surprised it hadn't already. She took a few pictures of the new growth. It was one of her favourite things to photograph, nature strangling and devouring something manmade—reclaiming it as hers again. Mother nature just didn't give a fuck and Ruth loved it.

She noticed Ria didn't take many pictures. She spent a long time standing at the altar, looking up at the half-decrepit statue of Jesus on a cross, mouth slack with two-thousand-year old agony. The whole thing looked like it might come down at any second.

'Crucifixes have always creeped me out,' Ruth said, stepping up beside her. 'So morbid.'

'Is that God?'

'No. His kid.' Ruth smiled. 'You grow up under a rock?'

'Close.' Ria raised her camera and took a picture. 'Who

did that to him?'

'His fellow man. Who else?' Ruth reached out and touched the hair that fell down Ria's back. It almost blended into the thermal top that was tucked into belted jeans. Reaching a hand to her own head, she took off her beanie and placed it on Ria's head, rearranging the hair falling over her temples. It made her less spy-assassin and more grunge. 'God, you look hot in that.'

Ria raised an eyebrow. 'God? Can you summon him with a name?'

Ruth chuckled. 'You are so weird.' She stepped forward and kissed Ria on the lips, her camera pressed between their bodies. If the crucifix was going to come tumbling down, it would be now. She wasn't normally the superstitious type but…Tucking her fingers into the waistband of Ria's jeans, she guided her down the steps and backed her into a pillar, away from the crucifix.

With impatient hands, Ria shoved the camera over her back and gripped the hair at the nape of Ruth's hair, tugging hard and running the tip of her tongue quickly over her bottom lip before biting down. *God*. Ruth huffed out a gust of air through her nose. So urgent. Did the girl ever take a break? Ruth always thought she had a healthy sex drive, but this girl…shit.

She pulled back, smiling when Ria's gaze darkened at her inability to reach her. 'This is still a church…'

'Help me understand,' Ria said.

'It might be abandoned but a house of God is a house of God.' Ruth pressed a kiss to her neck. 'Most would consider this to be disrespectful.'

'Best to not offend your God, then.' Ria put a hand flat to Ruth's chest and gently pushed her away, eyes lit with amusement.

'You are such a tease,' Ruth murmured, letting Ria move out from in front of her. 'Got all the snaps you want?' Ria nodded once. 'Cool, let's move on then.'

'To where?'

'Couple of other places I want to show you.'

They exited the chapel and travelled further into the forest.

'Just down here,' Ruth said, throwing out a hand to indicate the path, 'there's some factories. Super out of the way so a good place to come to. Some are still being used but the ones at the back shut years back.' Ruth glanced at Ria to see if she was listening and caught the end of a less-than-sure nod. 'You still into this? We can bail if not. Go do something else.'

Ria met her eyes. 'No,' she said. 'I want you to show me your world.'

Ruth grinned at that. Her world. Her dark, grotty underworld littered with needles and pigeon shit. For once, she was happy to be showing it to someone else. 'Alright. Although this might be less quaint than a little chapel in the woods.'

When Ruth spotted the grey of buildings up ahead, she took Ria's hand and guided her off the path. 'Just have to sneak around here.' They crossed a narrow access road and arced around the cluster of factories it led to.

There was nothing but trees for a time, though Ruth could hear the beeping of vehicles backing up behind them, and the clanging of machinery. When those noises fell away, the trees opened onto a broken concrete path lining a grimy, dilapidated building. Most of its window panes had been smashed in, glass littering the ground at their feet, and the metal stairs snaking around its walls were brown with rust.

'Here we are.' Ruth flicked her eyes around, searching for any other signs of life. They seemed to be alone. Still holding Ria's hand, she rounded a corner. 'Shit.' She looked up and down the bordered-up door then gave it a useless shove with her toe. 'This used to be open.' She pulled on Ria's hand. 'Let's try around here.'

All the ground floor windows were bordered up but Ruth found one where the board was loose and could be moved enough to fit through a person. 'Someone must have done this recently.' She turned to Ria. 'Want to go first?'

There wasn't much on Ria's face to give away how she felt but Ruth was pleased when she dropped her hand and squeezed through the gap without comment.

This particular factory was pretty sparse apart from the machinery shoved to one side of it. The ground floor was dark from the covered windows but the upper walkway was bright, the missing windows allowing for a small breeze to enter and blow autumn leaves down to them.

'What was made here?' Ria asked, eyes lingering on the huge hunks of metal, formidable in the dim. Her fingers were absently playing with the beanie still on her head, pulling it further and further down until the bottom of it sat just above her eyes.

'Dunno,' Ruth replied, taking a picture. She stood just far enough away from Ria that she could get her in the shot and she brought up the picture on the screen afterwards, liking how Ria looked nothing more than a shadow in it.

'If we go up another floor,' she told her, 'there's some pretty cool graffiti. Just have to watch the floor. My friend said it's fallen through in places.'

They found some stairs in a corner and ascended to the walkway, traversing across it carefully and passing through to the next room. There were chunks missing from this floor, great gaping gaps showing the tops of the machinery from the floor below. Rusted metal beams stretched over it and halfway across was a plastic bag and an empty two litre bottle of cider. Ruth wondered who had been here before them, and what they had been thinking about as they sat here alone, dangling their legs over the beam.

'You okay?' Ruth asked, noticing that Ria had halted her progress across the room. She seemed to have forgotten she'd brought her camera; she hadn't taken it out once.

Ria nodded. 'Just feeling the beginnings of a headache.'

'Ah, that's shit. We won't stay long then. Just want to get a few pics from up here.'

Quickly but carefully, Ruth edged further into the room,

crouching down to angle her camera at a wall of graffiti lit by the broken windows. It was a colourful piece, way out of place, but Ruth liked the contrast.

She was aware of Ria following her and lowered her camera to say something when an almighty crash made her jump to her feet. She whirled to where Ria stood, staring down through a new gap in the floor. One hand was clasped around a thick chain hanging from the ceiling, her feet sticking out an inch over the hole.

'Your friend was right,' she said calmly, backing up and toeing her way back to Ruth.

'*Fuck*.' Ruth clutched her camera and gave a breathless chuckle. 'That could have gone so bad.'

By silent agreement, they made their way back to the ground floor, stepping over ceiling shards.

'One more place,' Ruth said. 'Then we'll make tracks.'

Ria nodded, ushering her on. They left the factory, wending round to a side they hadn't ventured yet. There was a small building a few paces away, maybe used for storage, Ruth wasn't sure. It had no windows and no doors, so was easily accessible. Ruth stepped up to what would have been a doorway, eyes unable to penetrate the murky darkness.

Ruth had only been inside once before and she had been thankful Jed had tagged along with her because the interior was spooky as fuck. They'd found a pig's head—an honest to god head of a pig—perched on a chunk of broken wall. Jed reckoned it was some kind of practical joke and Ruth hoped he was right because the rest of the place wasn't much better. Under torchlight, the tiled walls were white, but written all over them in some kind of drippy red liquid were a whole bunch of—well—confessions was what they were. Phrases like *Please forgive me* and *I'm sorry* and on and on. It'd given Ruth the creeps big time and she'd vowed never to step place in the building again. And yet here she was, with Ria—

'Go in,' she said, nodding her head at the archway.

Ria peered in. 'Why?' She sounded dubious.

'Just 'cause.' Ruth folded her arms. 'Initiation.'

Ria gave her a brief searching look before crossing the threshold. Ruth opened her mouth, about to offer her a light but then closed it again. Ria had already disappeared.

She kept her eyes on the archway, hearing the scuffs of Ria's shoes as she wandered around. She wondered if the phrases were still on the walls. She wondered how Ria could see.

Her thoughts turned inward. Was she trying to put Ria off? No, she didn't think it was that. More like she wanted to put her through her paces, try and shake up her rod-straight, cool façade. She got a glimpse of something wilder when they were in bed together, when she bared her teeth as she reached the cusp, when she watched Ruth race towards that point herself. She liked that Ria. That Ria could hold her attention. She wanted to see more of her.

And…there was something else too. Something about Ria that made her almost—angry wasn't the right word, but it was close. It was a tiny flare in her stomach that made her want to grit her teeth, want to…She didn't know. She wasn't sure where the feeling came from. It was too disconcerting to think much about.

The building was only small and it didn't take Ria long to circle it. When she returned, Ruth expected her to look the least bit disturbed, but her face was as impassive as ever, one eyebrow raised slightly as if to say *yeah, now what?*

Ruth shook her head. 'So unruffled.' She cupped her hands around Ria's cheeks and kissed her, deeply but briefly. Then she slung an arm around her shoulders and turned them in the direction of the forest path.

'Come on. Let's head.'

CHAPTER 14

Ruth grabbed the support on the seat in front of her as the bus took another bumpy turn around a corner. She glanced at Ria, noticing the glaze in her eyes as she stared out of the window. She hadn't said a word since they'd boarded.

Ruth nudged her. 'Hey, how's that headache?'

'Bad.'

Ria's jaw was tightly clamped and she looked about ready to hurl. Ruth laid a hand on her thigh.

'Do you want to come back to mine? My stop is next. My place isn't far.'

When Ria nodded, Ruth reached out to press the bell. Cautiously, Ria followed her to the front of the bus and when they stepped down onto the street, Ruth took her hand and guided her along the short walk back to her flat.

'Just through here,' she said, pushing open the door. 'Go sit on the sofa. I'll get you some painkillers.'

When Ruth returned to her with a glass of water and paracetamol, Ria had taken off the beanie and laid slouched against the sofa, one hand gripping the hair at the top of her head. It put her facial features into sharp focus and although she looked sickly as hell, Ruth couldn't help but ogle a little.

'Here.' She passed the glass over and put the pills down on the coffee table. 'Turned into a migraine, hasn't it?' She sat down beside her. 'They suck. Well, you're welcome to chill here until it passes.'

Releasing her hair, Ria sipped the drink, ignoring the pills entirely. Wanting to be of more help, Ruth put a hand to the back of her neck and massaged. 'Wanna go to my room?' she said. 'It'll be cosier there. You can sleep it off. Only thing that works for me when I get them.'

In the bedroom, Ruth offered Ria an oversized t-shirt to change into but it was waved off. She pointed to the bed. 'Get under.'

Watching Ria get comfortable, she thought back to the last time she'd laundered her sheets. Two days ago. Good. She crossed to the window and pulled closed the curtains. The window was cracked open slightly, the burr of car engines and impatient beeps trickling in. When Ruth turned back to the bed, Ria was watching her from under the covers, her eyes open a slit. Ruth smiled, joining her on the other side of the bed, stretching out her legs on top of the covers and leaning back against the headboard.

'I'll put a film on or something. You don't have to watch if it hurts your head.'

She picked up her laptop from where she'd negligently left it on the floor and balanced it on her lap. When she had the film running—something quiet, something slow—she peeked down at Ria again. She had her eyes closed and the furrow in her forehead had smoothed out some. Ruth reached down, cupping a palm around her head and massaging gently with her fingers. Ria murmured, making Ruth smile.

This was new. This was…intimate. More intimate even than when they slept together. People who just 'hung out' didn't do this. But Ruth just shrugged to herself. She didn't care right now. She liked this feeling, the feeling of being the one at the helm. She didn't wish migraines on anyone but Ria's mask had slipped somewhat, she wasn't the one calling the shots right now and it made her seem more…human.

During the course of the film, Ruth found herself sliding down the headboard until she too was lying down. She glanced at Ria who was still conked and smothering a yawn, and then she placed the laptop back down on the floor. She stretched out her body before turning and curling up on her side, forming a moon shape with Ria. Her eyes closed a second later.

When they opened again, unknown moments later, Ria's eyes were open and boring into hers. Ruth blinked.

'Wow, hi. Feeling better?'

'Much.' Ria's voice was groggy from sleep. She cleared her throat.

'Good. Knew a nap would do it.' She glanced at the clock on her bedside table, noting it was now early evening. 'Don't know about you but I'm bloody starving. Wanna get food? I can deliver it here.'

'I would like that.' Almost gingerly, Ria sat up. Her hair was tousled, wild around her face and her eyes were still glassy from sleep.

Ruth had seen Ria just after she'd slept, but it was different somehow, her waking up in her bed. She felt almost proud to have such a stunning thing tucked up between her sheets. She had the childish urge to phone Sheila and say *see, see!* Instead, she found herself reaching over, placing a kiss to Ria's temple. Her hair smelled of green things, of damp things. It wasn't dissimilar to the musty scent from the chapel.

'I'll just get my phone,' Ruth said quietly.

Half an hour later, Ruth walked into the kitchen with a brown bag of food in her hand, to see Ria was sat at the small dining table, straight-backed and bright-eyed. Ruth began divvying out the food and couldn't help but notice how Ria's brow furrowed as she eyed the spread.

'What?' Ruth asked, removing the lid from a chicken salad. 'This not what you ordered?'

'No, it's just…I just didn't take you as someone who cared for…fresh things.'

Ruth smiled, sitting down. 'Yeah, I never used to be a health freak. I'm still not, really. I'm just on a bit of a health kick. For head reasons.'

'Head reasons?'

'Yeah, the old mental health's been a bit shit for a while. Well, more shit than usual. It's kind of another reason why dating right now is out of the question.'

Ria was quiet for a moment, moving a spear of asparagus around with her fork. Ruth moved her gaze away from her, concentrating on her meal. It was none of Ria's business really, but since they weren't dating, Ruth didn't really care about putting her off, or running the risk of 'trauma bonding' or any of that shit. She just felt like being honest and didn't think that was a bad thing.

'What happened to you to cause this state of mind?' Ria finally asked.

That made Ruth pause. She stopped chewing, throwing her mind back one year, two years, but everything was all kind of soupy.

'Dunno, just life I guess.'

Her fork tapped restlessly against the side of her salad container.

'Sometimes I get—I dunno, just really down with it all. Like, I don't have much going on. All I do is work so I can pay the rent on this place. But I never save anything. I hardly ever see friends unless I'm on shift with them. And then when I do finally get a day off, I spend the whole time having some kind of existential crisis.' Ruth paused before finishing off with, 'And I make really, really crap decisions.' She nodded. 'So there, that's me and my shitty life in a nutshell. *Bon appétit.*' Ruth looked at Ria, gauging her reaction to her spiel. Well, she didn't look put off. There was concern there and it looked pretty genuine. Ruth found herself wanting to comfort her. 'Don't worry about it. I got the self-care thing down.' She grinned, trying to lighten the mood. 'If you stay until morning, I can make you one of my smoothies.'

Ria smiled but Ruth knew it was only because it was expected of her.

'I know a little of what it's like not to own your own life.' Ruth held Ria's eyes, silently bidding her to go on. 'My father. He is a—leader. He has quite a number of people under his administration.'

'Like he owns a business?'

Ria inclined her head. 'And after he steps down, he wishes me to take his place. Me, as opposed to my sisters.'

'And you don't want to.'

A little shake of Ria's head. 'I do not. I hope to be struck down before then.'

Ruth mulled that over a little. 'Well, a family business means you'll always have money, I guess. Even if you hate it. You have that kind of security not everyone else has.'

Ria cocked her head. 'Is that what you seek, Ruth? Stability, security?'

'Well, yeah. Don't we all?'

'But what of other things? That kind of life, it leaves no room for—for passion, for experience. For…love.'

Ruth sighed. 'This is really depressing me.' She showed a palm. 'That's just my life, okay?' She felt tears prick at her eyes. She dropped her fork, bored of the food. When Ria gave her a pained, pitying look, she changed the subject. 'What does your dad do anyway? What's his business?'

'People. People are his business.'

'What, like HR kind of thing?'

'If you wish.'

'Sounds dull.'

Ria gave a humourless smile. 'Sometimes. But, Ruth, what I mean to say is—we're similar, you and I. We understand each other.'

Ruth shook her head slowly. 'I'm not sure about that.'

Ria looked away, sighing. She pressed the tips of two fingers to her forehead in a gesture of agitation. When she lowered them, her face was smooth again. 'What would you prefer to be doing?' she pressed. 'If you could.'

'My photos,' Ruth replied immediately but quietly. 'I have so many and I have this editing software now and I don't think they're amazing or anything, but they're not bad. Some of them I post to this forum but most are just sitting on my laptop not doing anything.'

'If those are what brings you joy, then that should be your focus.' Ria's voice was just as quiet but no less passionate.

Ruth shrugged. 'But how though?'

'An exhibition. This city isn't short of them. You just have to find one. Come on Ruth.' Ria's eyes narrowed and Ruth was reminded of a predator again. 'I know there's a fire in you. I know it hasn't been extinguished.'

No, not extinguished—not quite. An ember was still there, a minute light smothered by layers of dirt and leaves, but still there and it was like Ria—her words—was cupping her hands around it, breathing it back to a flame.

'I'll look into it then,' she said, and she knew she would.

CHAPTER 15

Ruth beeped the horn of the car again, this time holding her hand down to demonstrate her impatience. The car she was idling in was Sheila's and it was freezing. She cranked the heating up to high, catching sight of Sheila finally emerging from the pub.

'Took your damn time,' Ruth said, pulling away from the curb once Sheila had buckled herself in.

'Yeah, yeah. Just keep your eyes on the road.'

Ruth did. It was a treat to drive Sheila's car. She'd passed her test a good while ago but her paltry wage stopped her from getting a car of her own and Sheila felt it was important to keep up with it. So she let Ruth ferry her to and from doctor's appointments—hospital appointments, too, when needed. Her chest had been giving her gyp lately and she was currently being tested for a bunch of stuff.

'So. Dare I ask how your love life is going?'

Ruth smiled. 'Pretty good. Not sure how much love there is though.'

'So you're—what is it? Friends with benefits?'

Ruth gave a half nod. 'I just like hanging out with her. And yeah, that stuff's good too.'

'Judging by the shit-eating grin on your face just now, I'd say it's more than good.'

Ruth laughed. 'Maybe. We're just compatible in that way. Like majorly. I have orgasms every time with her. Like every time. That never happens.'

'Honey, I'm on the other side of menopause here. I don't need to be hearing about your orgasms.'

Ruth knitted her brows. 'What, you can't have orgasms after menopause?'

Sheila rolled her eyes. 'Lord, give me strength.' She sighed. 'I'm just happy you're happy, doll.'

Ruth grinned. 'Happy and jealous.'

'Am not.'

'Then stop fishing for the juicy stuff.'

Sheila fell silent as Ruth turned a corner, merging onto the road which would take her to the hospital.

'Ruthie.'

'Mm?' Ruth kept her eyes on the road, slowing down as a kid jumped off the curb to retrieve an errant football.

'This appointment might take a while so I want you to go occupy yourself until I'm done. No point sitting in the waiting room, bored to death for an hour.'

Ruth frowned. 'An hour? Everything okay? Thought it was just a check-up.'

'It is—mostly. Just don't want you to be bored, that's all.'

Ruth nodded and turned into the carpark. She shut off the engine and turned to Sheila. 'Sure you don't want me to come in with you?'

'No, chuck. Go grab a coffee or something. I'll let you know when I'm done.' She left the car, slamming the door shut and rapping her knuckles on the window before disappearing into the hospital.

Ruth sat for a moment, tapping her thumbs on the steering wheel and worrying the inside of her lip. *Hm.* She unclipped her seatbelt and got out the car, wandering over to the ticket machine. That sorted, she gave one last suspicious look in the direction of where Sheila had gone and then left the carpark.

She wandered mostly aimlessly, in the vague direction of the small shopping area they'd driven past on the way. It was almost Halloween and most of the shop windows were shrouded in artificial cobwebs. Ruth paused outside a costume shop before ducking into it. Despite being the one to decorate the pub, she hadn't given much thought to what she'd be doing for the holiday. She was working on actual Halloween night but figured most people would be celebrating the weekend prior. She was supposed to be going to a party with Molly but obviously that wasn't happening. She wondered if Ria…

She picked up a tub of white face paint, turning it over in her hands. She was never one to go full-out for Halloween but the pale, blood-stained look never went amiss. She claimed a tube of fake blood next and a black, gothic choker which would look great around Ria's throat. She could envision her going as a vampire or something. Maybe even Morticia Addams, or Dracula's bride. Ruth smiled. She didn't even have anywhere to go yet but was already planning their night.

Things had been going pretty well after their date at the factories. If you could call it a date. Ria had spent a couple of nights at Ruth's; she seemed to prefer that than staying at hers. Ruth didn't have a problem with that but she couldn't deny that Ria's bed was way comfier.

She'd come to enjoy their morning routine of watching explorer videos on YouTube in bed, breakfast smoothies in hand. The one time she'd asked Ria to choose something, they'd ended up watching some documentary on human evolution. It'd bored her at first and she couldn't help but rib Ria for her choice, but soon she was so wrapped up in it, she'd almost made herself late for work.

Ruth left the costume shop and crossed the road to the coffee shop she'd had her eye on. It looked pretty cool inside, lots of plants and neon lights and there was some kind of art gallery attached to it. As she walked up to the counter, she peered at the photos from a distance—a mix of city landscape and portrait photography. It all looked local.

She quickly rattled off her order to the barista and

looked back at the gallery, an idea forming. As she waited for her drink, her phone buzzed in her pocket. She pulled it out, seeing a text from Ria.

I thought you might like this.

Ruth opened the attached photo, lips already curled into a smile. It was a picture of a wall, covered in trailing ivy and yellow-grey lichen. Sitting against it on the pavement was a doll with one eye missing and half of its plastic skull caved in. It listed sideways like it might fall at any second. Ruth smoothed a thumb over the doll.

I love it, she replied. *Also, I think I've got an idea. Are you free on Halloween?*

CHAPTER 16

The streets were teeming with all manner of monster and man. So far Risarial had passed ghosts and vampires and other half-dead creatures. She wondered if she slipped her glamour now, would anyone even notice? It was a strange celebration, Halloween. For a night, it was as if the veil between the human realm and Risarial's court slipped away. She knew the Exiled would be out roaming tonight, using the celebration to walk among humans undetected. She must ensure she remained undetected herself. She'd been— wobbly, lately, more so than usual, and it had taken more attention than normal to remain glamoured. Especially after her and Ruth's escapade to the factories the other week. Risarial grimaced, remembering the ensuing migraine. She mentally apologised to Ruth because—Ruth be damned— she would never step foot in such a dank, fetid place again. Not in the name of love, not for anything. All that iron…she could still feel the phantom of that headache, pulsing at the back of her eyes.

She'd been in such situations before, of course. Some discomfort was expected if one ventured earthside, but she'd always bounced back once removed from whatever was making her ill. This time though, she was still besieged with the odd bout of nausea and dizziness so strong she often had to stop whatever she was doing to take stock of her glamour.

She still scolded herself for remaining at Ruth's after the

factories. Simply a foolish, reckless thing to do. She was in pain though, desperately, and just wanted comfort. She'd woken after her foggy migraine slumber, Ruth lying inches from her, with the terrible realisation that her glamour had peeled away. By some grace, Ruth was asleep and hadn't noticed. She let the glamour wash over her again and spent the next half an hour watching that beautiful human and thanking her stars that Ruth hadn't awoken before her. She only hoped the sickness would pass and that she wouldn't need to flee home in order to restore her health.

Tonight wasn't the time to worry about such things though. Tonight, as per Ruth's request, she was begowned in a long black dress. It was one from home, the one she'd left buried beneath the boulder. She'd slogged through miles of rain and mud to get it back, wanting its comfort as she was reminded of a previous Halloween and everything that had gone wrong then.

She forced herself to cease thinking such things as Ruth's pub came into view. She stepped up to the doorway and into the fug of music and alcohol and hot, human breath. Manoeuvring past people in costumes, she made her way to the bar.

Ruth's ward was standing behind it. She knew Sheila wouldn't remember her from last time, she'd made sure of that, but she still noted some suspicion in the woman's eyes as she asked for Ruth.

'She's just out back. Be round in a minute,' Sheila said. Her short, spiky hair reminded Risarial of a hedgehog but she didn't think that was her costume as she also wore a pair of black, cat-like ears.

'She's been looking forward to tonight, Ruth has,' the woman went on. Still, the suspicion was there.

'As have I,' Risarial said.

As she regarded the woman, she became aware of something heavy, something insidious pulsating inside of Sheila. Risarial let her eyes drop to the woman's chest, then back up to her grey eyes. Did Sheila know of the cancer growing inside her? Did Ruth?

'You know it's her birthday in a couple of days, don't you? Halloween,' Sheila said, breaking eye contact. Risarial did know, because it was on Ruth's birthday, at another Halloween party, that— 'Doubt she would've told you. Likes to keep that crap on the lowdown. I'm not saying you have to or anything but might be nice to do something for her, you know? I'm here working and I don't really want her on her own until her shift.'

Risarial nodded. She needn't be told. She turned away from the bar slightly, eyeing the direction she hoped Ruth would appear from.

'Hey, Ria ain't it?' Risarial turned back reluctantly. 'Look, I'm not her mother or anything but it needs to be said, I think. I know she acts all tough and that, but she's been through the right ringer that one and just needs a gentle hand now. You're a couple years older, aren't you?' Risarial inclined her head without comment.

'Yeah, well.' Sheila began walking away, saying quietly, 'She's vulnerable, that's all I'm saying.'

A small kernel of anger welled at those words. Stupid woman. She didn't need to be warned. Risarial knew of Ruth's vulnerabilities, knew all of her hurts, her torments, her—

'Hey.' Risarial was jostled out of her thoughts by Ruth bumping her hip. 'Look at you,' she crooned, eyeing Risarial up and down. 'Damn.'

Risarial smirked, pursing her lips as she surveyed Ruth in turn. She had on a ripped blouse, speckled with red stains, a painted white face and black lipstick.

'I've got some stuff for you,' Ruth continued. She took the stool next to Risarial, placing some items on the bar in front of them. 'First, this.' Risarial glanced at the thing in her hands; a black velvet choker with a silver cross hanging from it. Holding still, she let Ruth put her hands around her neck and fasten it. 'And now your face.' She picked up a tub of white. 'You're a vampire tonight, okay?'

'And what are you?'

A devilish glint came into Ruth's eyes. 'Your human blood slave.' She waved a hand in front of her face. 'Hence the bloodless look. Now, close your eyes. I don't wanna get this stuff in them.'

Risarial did as bade, letting Ruth dab the cold, damp sponge along her skin. Trying not to flinch, she drew in a long breath and let it out, settling into the darkness in front of her eyelids. Ruth was gentle, cupping her chin in one hand loosely, the other running in long, slow rivulets along the planes of her face. Every so often the thumb of the hand holding her chin would stroke her jaw, sending a bolt straight to the point between her legs. She knew under her eyelids, her irises would be orange.

When Ruth's hands fell away, she finally opened her eyes but Ruth wasn't finished yet. She reached for a tube of fake blood, uncapping the lid, and slid close to Risarial again. Risarial kept her eyes open this time, letting herself study the minute flickers of Ruth's eyelids, the dark specks in her eyes, the smoothness of her painted skin.

'Stop looking at me like that,' Ruth whispered, without looking up, smearing the fake blood over her lips and chin.

Risarial smiled, glancing away, her eyes meeting Sheila's over Ruth's shoulder. The woman looked at her without feeling and Risarial stared back until she turned away.

'All done.' Ruth sat back up. 'Hey Sheila, can I dump this stuff here?' Sheila waved a hand at her. 'Sweet.' Ruth turned to Risarial. 'Let's go then.'

❧ ❧

'It's one of those secret location, you don't know where it is until the night things,' Ruth was saying as they wended their way through a woodland. They'd gotten a taxi to a housing estate on the outskirts of the city and had been walking away from it since. 'No doubt the police will come fuck things up though,' Ruth continued, 'hence why we're

96

going kind of early.'

Ruth glanced at her phone again. She had a map up, checking they were still heading in the right direction. Any lights had since fallen away and they walked in pitch blackness apart from the torchlight from Ruth's phone.

She shined it in Risarial's direction. 'I've got booze in my bag. Did you bring any?' When Risarial shook her head, she gave an exaggerated sigh. 'Lucky I brought enough for the both of us then, isn't it?'

'I hear music,' Risarial said, sniffing the air is if it made her hear better.

'Do you?' Ruth listened in silence for a few moments. 'I don't.'

'It's up ahead.'

A few minutes later and the music was loud enough for even Ruth to hear. 'Shit, you've got super hearing.' Ruth grinned as the trees fell away and the location was finally revealed. 'Oh my god, this is better than I thought it would be.'

Standing in a muddy clearing scattered with building equipment was a large, three-story house. Most of the windows were either boarded up or covered in plastic sheets but the front doors stood wide and dry smoke was blowing through them, toying with the ankles of people coming in and out of the house. Like them, most people were dressed in costumes. Risarial ran a quick eye around. They were all human.

'Bet you anything the police will be here within the hour,' Ruth said. 'Come on, let's make the most of it.'

They followed a group of boys dressed in brightly coloured, full-body suits up the front steps and into the entry hall. There were no bulbs in any of the ceiling lights but narrow strips of ultraviolet tubing lined the ceilings, vying with the fitful party lights. Over the walls were painted symbols—bats and ghosts and upside down crosses. They all glowed under the UV lights.

Over the sound of the loud, bassy music, Risarial heard

Ruth say, 'This is mint!'

They passed through into a larger room where most of the revellers were gathered. A long, wide table sat in the middle of the room, holding an array of drinks, most canned and bottled, others pooled in glass bowls, like the punch served at court gatherings. In the corner were hunks of black machinery where Risarial guessed the music came from.

Risarial crossed to the table, plucked a red, plastic cup and dunked it into the punch.

'Don't be an idiot, Ria,' Ruth admonished. 'You'll be drugged to fuck if you drink that.'

Risarial raised the cup to her nose and sniffed. She smelt nothing too nefarious within it, just a more-than-healthy serving of distilled alcohol and whatever artificial flavourings were in the juice. She took a sip, causing Ruth to shake her head. 'Well, I promise not to take advantage of you when you're paralytic later.' Her fingers reached up to play with the choker around Risarial's neck. 'Or maybe I will.'

Ruth took off her backpack, grabbed a cup and began decanting from two bottles into it. 'Can we go outside?' she shouted over the music. 'Wanna talk a sec.'

Risarial followed her into the back garden, finding a quiet spot on the deck. They leant against the wooden rail. On the barely lit grass in front of them, a girl in fishnet tights and red devil horns jumped onto a boy's back. The boy span in a circle, making the girl lose her drink. She shrieked just before they hit the ground, where they lay laughing on the grass. The girl turned over and kissed the boy.

'So,' Ruth said, turning to address her. There was a light in her eyes that made Risarial hold her breath. She hadn't seen that light since their reunion. Hadn't realised how much she missed it. 'I did what you said. I found a gallery to show my stuff.' Risarial's lips pulled up into a smile. 'It's only small but…It's their Halloween showing. They said my stuff is spooky enough and it's local, which they liked.'

'That's incredible, Ruth.'

Ruth nodded, looking away, lips tucked in. 'Yeah, I'm pretty chuffed. Will you come? It's on Halloween.'

'Your birthday.' At Ruth's frown, she said, 'That woman—Sheila told me.'

'Oh. Yeah it is, but—' Ruth waved her hand. 'So will you come?'

'I will come and,' Risarial reached out and cupped her face, 'we will celebrate your birthday.'

Ruth rolled her eyes. 'If we must. I don't usually do anything for it. It's kind of—well, it's never been a big deal. My family, they—I don't want to get into it but basically it's never been great.'

I know, Risarial wanted to say, watching the girl's expression shutter. *I know how your father left you. I know how your mother hates you because you remind her of him. I know how your brother pretends you don't exist. I know how you've been on your own until Sheila picked you up and set you on your feet. I know how your heart is still fractured. I know you, Ruth. I* know *you.*

Instead she said, 'It will be great this time.'

Ruth pitched forward, pressing her lips to Risarial's, causing her to bump back against the rail. When she pulled back a second later, there was something in her face that made Risarial's heart beat quicker. Ruth took her hand and smiled. 'Wanna go dance?'

Risarial nodded, letting herself be pulled back inside.

❧ ❧

Risarial had her eyes closed, multicoloured lights playing on the insides of her eyelids, head thrown back slightly. Every so often she'd feel hands—Ruth's hands—graze her waist, her stomach, her shoulders and she'd reach out, fingers tucking into the rips in Ruth's shirt as their hips bumped.

Courtiers didn't dance like this. Nor the Gentry, not in her world. Only the underclass would move like this—

writing, swaying like wild beasts. If her father saw her now…Risarial smiled. Her exile wouldn't be all that terrible, not now that she had Ruth again.

'What are you smiling at?' Ruth said into her ear.

Risarial cracked open her eyes. 'How you lower my inhibitions like no other.'

Ruth smiled back, clearly pleased. 'Well, you're welcome,' she mouthed back, words lost to the music. She leaned back in and said, 'I'm going to find a toilet. Don't go anywhere.'

Risarial accepted the cup Ruth thrust at her, moving backwards into a quiet corner where she could watch the room with eyes at half slit. Most of the revellers were young—Ruth's age or thereabouts, though a few seemed older, more out of place. In front of the human playing the music was a rail-thin man, dressed in a hooded jacket, face obscured. He didn't have a drink in his hand but his body moved jerkily, a beat or two quicker than the music playing. A group of teenagers stood behind him, mimicking his movements and laughing.

Her eyes moved on, capturing those of another man leaning against the wall opposite hers. The lights didn't reach there and he stood in a pocket of shadow. He was maybe as old as Sheila, bald and stern-looking. Risarial maintained his gaze for a moment longer before moving on and that was when she saw it—saw *them*.

Her fingers stiffened around the cup in her hand and she felt herself take in a quick breath through her nose. Her reality swam and suddenly she was at another Halloween revel, desperately imploring a devastated Ruth, and trying to quell the murderous itch in her heart.

From the archway, the redcap grinned and the itch was back. The exiled creature was glamoured but Risarial glimpsed the creature behind it, like peering through a gap in a door into the room beyond. Through her tiny body, straggly short hair and human clothing, Risarial could see the needle-sharp teeth and brown, leathery skin. Though she would look mostly human to anyone passing her, her glamoured features were all off—eyes too circular, grin too wide.

Risarial let Ruth's drink fall to the floor and took a step towards the redcap, just as Ruth appeared in the doorway beside them. Risarial could have cursed herself for glancing her way because the redcap's gaze joined hers, eyes widening at seeing the same human.

Risarial pitched forward but she knew she wouldn't make it in time, she was paces away from them. The redcap moved an instant after she did and Risarial saw a glint of claws at her fingertips. Heavens, she was going to do it, she was going to kill—

'POLICE!'

The music stopped and the sudden stillness in the room gave Risarial the advantage she needed. She grabbed Ruth, pulling her away from the redcap and towards the back of the house where everyone now fled.

'Ow, shit Ria!' Ruth protested, breath stuttering in her chest. 'Calm down. Ria!' Risarial glanced at her, then behind them. She couldn't see the redcap but suddenly she could see other fae, dotted in between the humans, wild grins on their faces as they ran amongst them, wolves in sheepskins.

'Ria, chill.' Ruth was laughing at her, breathless from running. They were in the woods now, following the adrenaline-fueled screeches of the revellers around them. 'I don't think they're gonna get us. Slow down, will ya. I need to figure out where we are.'

Ruth dropped her hand and slowed down enough to take her phone out and Ria wanted to scream at her.

Through laboured breaths, she scanned the trees. She couldn't see the house now, only the blackness of the woods spanning in all directions.

Ruth grabbed her hand again and turned them away from where everyone else was running. 'This way. It's quicker.'

'Ruth, no—'

'Trust me!' She lowered her voice. 'And shut up. Doubt the police will bother looking in the woods but I don't wanna chance it.'

After glancing behind them to make sure nobody was following, Ruth turned on her phone torch. 'This will take us to an industrial site, just beside that housing estate. Hopefully there won't be fences or anything and we can just pass through.'

Risarial opened her mouth to answer when a wave of dizziness slammed into her. *Oh, not now. Please not now.*

'Hey…you okay?' Vaguely, Risarial felt a hand squeeze hers as she pulled the tattered threads of her glamour tighter. She couldn't lose it now, not in front of Ruth. 'Ria?'

The dizziness ebbed but when Risarial opened her eyes, her sight was wavy. 'I'm okay,' she whispered, beginning to move again.

'Hope it wasn't that punch,' joked Ruth.

Desperately, Risarial tried to concentrate on her surroundings. Though blurry, her eyesight was stronger than Ruth's but she'd be able to see even better if not for the glare from Ruth's phone. She tried opening her hearing instead. There was the crashing of branches and the odd laugh or scream in the distance—the humans, running away. But they weren't what she was looking for.

When she heard shuffling to her right, no more than a whistling of wind, and then another at her left, Risarial suddenly knew what it felt like to be hunted. Ruth couldn't see the shapes running past her, but Risarial could, just blurred shadows in her peripheries. The fae, rallied together, dipping in and out of the trees, crowding them then disbanding so they could run ahead. So they could cut them off.

'We can probably chill out now,' Ruth said, the words spoken so loudly they made her flinch. 'No way the police will come out this far.'

The human's voice at her side, so innocent, trusting, pierced something inside of Risarial. She set her jaw, breathing a steady breath through her nose, quelling the queasiness in her stomach. It was not going to end like this. She'd just gotten Ruth back, dammit.

Using all of her senses to ensure the fae were still up ahead and out of sight, she pulled on Ruth's hand, dragging her behind a tree.

Ruth let out a surprised huff. 'Well, hello,' she murmured, threading her arms around Risarial's neck.

Risarial closed her eyes, face in Ruth's neck, as she listened to the fae thudding their way back to them. She kissed Ruth's pulse point, arms reaching round her to wrap around the tree trunk. Summoning energy she wasn't sure she had, she let her glamour fall away from her hands, pinning Ruth harder so she wouldn't see.

'I need to kiss you,' Ruth said and Risarial obliged, pressing her lips to Ruth's just as a vine burst from each of her palms. The pain of it made her gasp and Ruth responded, pushing her hips into her as best she could. There was barely room to breathe between them but Risarial pressed her harder. This wouldn't work if Ruth kept moving.

She twined the vines around the tree trunk, tying her and Ruth to the tree and rendering them invisible. Her breath became shaky, stuttered. It took so much concentration to tend to Ruth, to keep her eyes closed, to listen for the fae. They were around them now, Risarial could hear the squelch of a boot pushing into mulch, feel the confusion as they looked around, sourcing them.

Please Ruth, she begged silently, *stay still, stay quiet.*

Risarial kissed her so deeply that Ruth had no choice but to surrender to it. If they weren't being hunted, Risarial's legs would be quivering for different reasons. Ruth hadn't kissed her this fervently since the last time they were together.

A crunch of leaves at her right and Risarial cracked her eyes open. The redcap was right there, *right there*. She was stripped of her glamour, a horrid, hobbling thing with bulging eyeballs and teeth like tiny tusks, protruding unevenly from between her lips. Those eyes roved from left to right, searching for them. Risarial saw her lip curl up into a sneer and after a few more moments of scouring, she let out a defeated snarl and bounded away with the rest of them.

Ruth jolted. 'What the fuck was that?'

She pushed Risarial from her and looked around.

'Come on,' she finally said. 'I'm freezing up.'

The woods finally spat them out into the industrial state that Ruth had mentioned. They walked along the road in silence, lurid orange streetlights lighting their way. There was no one around at this hour, all the factories were shuttered and the machinery and vehicles around them were empty shells.

Ruth was quiet. Risarial glanced at her. She was deep in thought, eyes far away, though she didn't look troubled and Risarial desperately, *desperately*, wanted to ask what was running through that beautiful skull of hers but she held back. She was too angry, heavens was she angry. That—that piece of *filth*. Risarial's palms tingled. What she wouldn't do to wrap a vine around that redcap's neck and tighten it until the horrid, blood-soaked cap popped from her head. But she knew she lacked the energy for anything right now, let alone that. She had barely found the strength inside her to reglamour her hands. What was *wrong* with her? Please, please don't be the metal sickness.

'Hey.' Ruth's voice pulled her out of her own misery and she looked at her, immediately softening at the smile on her face. 'Wanna come back to mine? Or yours, I don't mind.'

Oh, Ruth. Risarial took in a breath. 'I—I don't think I can do that.'

Ruth cocked her head. 'You okay?' She reached out and took her hand and feeling the wetness there, turned it over. 'You're bleeding,' she exclaimed. Risarial nodded and held out her other hand. 'Is this real blood?'

'From the tree,' Risarial said tiredly. 'There were nails.'

'Woah. That is some stigmata shit right there.' Ruth turned over her palms, seeming almost disappointed the cuts didn't come out the other side. 'Your blood looks black in this light,' she mused, running her thumbs in circles around the wounds, smearing the blood.

My blood is black. Risarial removed her hands, curling them into fists. *As is the rest of me.*

'Don't you need some kind of shot for something like that? Can't you get, like, rabies or something. Wait, it's not rabies. Tetanus!' Ruth smiled in triumph and Risarial saw the girl was still drunk.

Risarial shook her head. 'I just need to go home. Alone.' She glanced over Ruth's shoulder, the streetlights wavering. 'I'm not feeling too well.'

'Okay, well, I'll see you in a couple of days.' Ruth smiled unsurely, voice tapering higher at the end so it was posed more like a question.

A couple of days—the exhibition, Ruth's birthday. Risarial took a breath and nodded.

'Promise?' Ruth looked so earnest standing there, hands slipping into her pockets—a defensive gesture, eyes shadowed. *Vulnerable*, Sheila had said. She certainly looked that now.

But Risarial couldn't promise, her nature forbade it, so she said instead, 'Naught but death could keep me away.'

CHAPTER 17

Ruth lay in bed blinking drowsily for a whole minute before the day dawned on her and she threw her arms over her eyes, groaning. Her birthday. Right.

She glanced at the clock. 9:00am. She'd been twenty for a whole nine hours. Two hours, if she was to go by her actual time of birth. Her mum had said once that she'd been born around seven in the morning. Ruth shook her head, sitting up. She didn't want to think about her mum, about any of them, but it was inevitable on this day. In her wakening state, she'd heard her phone chime a few times but she refused to look, damning the hopeful flip in her stomach. *Maybe this year*, the flip said.

'Fuck off,' Ruth muttered, getting out of bed. The hope made her feel weak and she hated it. As far as she was concerned, her family was dead to her—as she was to them.

But then she remembered the exhibit, and with it Ria's presence, and for the first time in a couple of years she felt something akin to excitement. She could play at having a good day, if nothing else.

Feeling lighter, she picked up her phone. Sheila had texted her—*Happy birthday doll, give you a call later*. Ria had sent a photo—a chunk of low wall with an old grimy deflated birthday balloon sagging over it. There was no text with the image but Ruth appreciated the poetry of it and sent a smiley face back in reply.

She had a couple of hours before she needed to make

tracks so she took a leisurely shower and then a walk to the café up the road for a proper coffee. Since it was her birthday, she was able to snag a free pastry which perked her mood up even more.

Walking home and chewing on the pastry, her thoughts drifted to Ria. They were soft thoughts—new. Not unwelcome, but she wasn't sure when things had changed for her. Probably Ria's persistence more than anything but Ria really seemed to care, care about *her*. She couldn't work out if she felt the same back or that just some broken part of her was seeking the love Ria would probably offer her if she'd only let her.

Too heavy a thought for her birthday. She put some music on when she got back to her flat and poured herself some whiskey, a bottle she'd stolen from the pub. It was supposed to be the good stuff but it tasted like shit so she only poured herself about a finger's width worth, trying not to grimace as she sipped.

Turning up the music on her speakers and taking the tumbler of whiskey into the bedroom with her, she set about trying to decide what to wear to this exhibit. There were nerves in her stomach that she hoped the alcohol would extinguish. It wasn't a super professional affair but still, she wanted to look good. Wanted *Ria* to think she looked good. Ruth rolled her eyes at herself, revelling for a moment in the warmth in her stomach, a warmth that had nothing to do with the whiskey.

By the time she'd picked an outfit—her black work trousers with a dark teal satin shirt—and located her file of photos that she'd hastily had printed the day before, it was an hour and a half before the start of the exhibit. If she set off now, she'd have time to get there on the bus and set up in the little corner they'd allocated to her.

She sent Ria a quick text to say she was leaving, asking again when she thought she might arrive. Her last text had gone unanswered and she couldn't help the flare of worry that maybe she wouldn't come after all. *Stop being an insecure dick, Ruth. The girl promised.*

Shrugging on her leather jacket, she tucked the plastic wallet of photos under her arm and left the flat.

Ruth tacked her last photo to the wall and stood back, running her eyes over the placement of the rest of them. The corner they'd assigned to her was half lit up with pink neon light and half in shadow. Ruth liked the effect it had on her photos. They looked kind of grungy and cool.

She felt a zing of pride for the first time ever and it was so foreign to her that she just as quickly quashed it.

'Looks great.'

Ruth turned, gracing the manager of the café with a smile. She was a youngish woman, not much older than Ruth, and had that hipster look going which matched the ambience of the café. 'Thanks. I don't have that many to show.'

'Quality over quantity. We open the doors in ten. Come grab a coffee and have a little look around.'

Free coffee in hand, Ruth slowly perused the other artists. Now that she was here and set up, she didn't feel nervous at all. She told herself she didn't care what people thought of her photos, that she was just stoked to be here. She was kind of excited for Ria to get here though. She'd encouraged her after all, so it'd be nice for her to see the fruits of her labour.

Ruth returned to her corner and stood with her back against the wall, waiting for the doors to open. She checked her phone, holding in a sigh at the sight of no new messages. She was about to call when two girls walked up to her, smiling politely as they peered at her photos. She tucked her phone back into her pocket, trying to appear approachable. She'd try Ria later.

Risarial leaned heavily against the kitchen sink, eyes unfocussed on the gardens outside. Her glamour was wavering in and out just as her vision was. The oscillating was making her nauseous and her legs trembled horribly, barely holding her up.

She was sick. She was really, really sick. Deathly? She wasn't sure. What she was sure about, however, was that there was no way she was going to see Ruth today. Through her discomfort, her chest burned.

Oh, Ruth.

She was beyond hoping the human would forgive her for anything now, even the things she didn't know she had to forgive Risarial for.

She was cursed. Risarial snorted weakly at the thought. For all she knew, she was. She was hated enough, inside the court and out of it.

A cold shiver ran through her, lifting all the tiny hairs on her skin. The sensation was so strong it hurt. She leaned heavier against the sink, wondering if she was going to vomit. The steel of the sink burnt her and she moved trembling fingers from it, curling them around the marble countertop instead.

She licked her lips, tasting blood where they'd cracked. She needed to text Ruth, to call her, but her mind was slipping away. She didn't know where she was. The buildings in the distance were alien and everything smelled strange.

There was something she was trying to recall. Her mind flickered like an empty film reel. Risarial closed her eyes so tight that they hurt.

Focus. Heavens, focus.

Gasping, Risarial stumbled over to the island, hands grasping at her phone. The thing clattered away from her, thumping to the floor.

Slowly, she lowered herself to a stool and closed her eyes.

Ruth pulled the last photo from the wall and shoved it into the folder. At the door, the other artists congregated, finishing the last of the nibbles laid out for the public. She pushed passed them on the way out of the café, ignoring the manager gesturing her over.

Her bus was just pulling up at she got to the stop and she boarded, sitting heavily in the first seat. An old woman settled beside her, knocking Ruth's knees with her walking frame. Ruth gritted her teeth and shoved it back.

The bus pulled away and Ruth felt her lips tremble. She folded her arms and took a breath. She was fine. It didn't matter. Just a stupid exhibition, not that big of a deal. Ria probably just forgot. Ruth snorted softly. *No she fucking didn't. You know she didn't. She just didn't want to come because you're not worth—*

Ruth felt an elbow prod her.

'You alright, lovey?' the lady beside her asked.

Ruth nodded, hastily rubbing the tears from her cheeks, embarrassed when her affirmative hum turned into more of a whimper.

She turned further towards the window, noticing that they were coming up to the river crossing. A thought crossed her mind and she suddenly jumped up.

'Excuse me,' she mumbled, pushing past the woman just as the bus came to a stop.

She paused out on the pavement, taking a moment to reorientate herself before starting off in the direction of Ria's apartment building.

Anger and hurt grew with every step and she didn't take a moment to consider what she'd do if Ria wasn't in. A man was exiting the building just as she stepped up to it and she bolted forward to catch the door and slipped inside.

In the lift, she watched her reflection in the mirror, hating how red and wide her eyes were, like those of a wounded kid. Before she reached Ria's flat, she made sure to school her expression back to indifference.

The door was open. Ruth hesitated for only a moment before stepping up and rapping her knuckles against it. 'Ria? You in there?'

She heard a commotion, like overturned glass bottles, and put her face around the door. Ria was just rising from an island stool, one hand gripping the countertop. She was wearing a slinky satin dress and Ruth tried not to think about how hot she looked, staring into her strangely glassy expression instead.

Ruth folded her arms. 'So you are here then.'

'Ruth?'

'Yeah it's me.' She rolled her eyes. 'Remember?'

'Ruth, you can't be here.'

Ruth took a step forward. 'Why? Why didn't you— where were you? I was waiting for you.'

'I was taken ill,' Ria said quietly, measuredly.

'You could have texted. You look fine to me.' But she didn't, not really. Her cheeks were pinched red against the unnatural pallor of her face and she was still gripping the island surface. But Ruth was still so fucking *angry* that she didn't have it in her to ask about these things yet. 'You made today *shit*.' When Ria continued to stare at her from under heavy lids, Ruth threw up her hands. 'Well fucking say something!'

'Leave.'

'What?'

'Leave.' And then, 'Ruth…please.'

Without warning, Ria fell to the floor, a gasp leaving her mouth at the force of it.

'Shit.' Ruth dropped to her knees beside her, pulling hair away from her face. 'Ria. Fuck. What's wrong?'

Ria batted her away. 'No. No, no, please,' she whispered. 'Leave. Get…get *out*. Now.'

'Shit, I'm not leaving you like this. I think…I think you need an ambulance. Can you tell me what's wrong? Do you know?' Ruth put a hand in her pocket and gripped her phone but just as she was about to pull it out, Ria's hand clamped painfully around her wrist. 'Ow, Ria.' She looked into Ria's eyes, breath catching at how lucid they suddenly were.

'No…ambulance,' she bit out.

'Then what?'

Ria's eyes fluttered shut for a moment and she took two composing breaths before opening them again. She was about to pass out, Ruth could see it, and it freaked her the fuck out. 'Coordinates,' Ria breathed, releasing the grip on Ruth's wrist. Ruth pulled out her phone and with shaking hands, opened her notes app. With difficulty, Ria began uttering the coordinates and she dutifully tapped them in. When she next looked up, Ria was unconscious. 'Shit!' Ruth looked down at her phone. 'Shit, shit, shit!'

She copied the coordinates into her map app, shaking her head when they took her to some random wooded area outside the city. 'What…?' She looked at Ria again. She was still breathing, heavy ragged breaths, so she wasn't on the brink of death yet. But god, her face was getting paler, even the red in her cheeks was vanishing before her eyes. 'Fuck it.' She was going to call an ambulance.

But when she was about to press the call button, something happened. There was a strange wavering in the air, like heat over a radiator, and her gaze was drawn back to Ria. She frowned. There was a dark pulsing under her skin, like a black bruise erupting at the surface, but it was all over her, trailing like veins through her face, her neck, over her arms and legs.

Ruth jumped back, her heart suddenly beating so fast it made her head swim. She rounded the island, peeking round it just enough so she could see and not see at the same time. She didn't know what was going on, didn't know why Ria's skin was doing that. Was it some kind of internal bleeding, a rupture somewhere? God, it was awful. She glanced down at her legs which were the closest body part to her. The black stuff…it looked like *leaves*.

Her eyes jumped back to Ria's face and she barely stifled a scream at what she saw because it wasn't Ria's face anymore. It couldn't be. It was longer, angular, more sunken. Like a model's face yet features so exaggerated they looked inhuman. And her eyes were open. Only a crack, but they stared at Ruth. 'Get me help, Ruth.' Then they rolled back and she was unconscious again.

Ruth stayed where she was for a whole minute, trying to get a handle on the crawly, alien, *wrong* feeling suddenly prickling all over her. She looked around the flat dazedly, then back at the phone in her hands, before raising it on instinct and taking a photo. She backed up then, heading for the door and just as she reached it, she plucked Ria's flat keys from the hook and pulled the door closed, locking Ria in.

CHAPTER 18

Ruth climbed out of the taxi, eying the boundary of trees in front of her with trepidation. Behind her, the car executed a U-turn then peeled off and Ruth watched it disappear, stamping down the urge to wave it back.

She was nervous and that perturbed her.

Anxiety wasn't a familiar feeling to her. Anger, yes. Depression, without a doubt. Even on her best days, apathy was the word she would choose to best describe how she felt towards everything. But this—she didn't feel qualified for it.

She wished she'd charged her phone before going out that morning. She only had one bar left and her map app was glugging that. Without thinking too much, she zoomed in to where she was standing and set a route. When the robotic voice instructed her to move north, she stepped into the boundary of trees.

She wasn't too far from civilisation yet and for that, she was glad. There was a main road running on the other side of her and though she couldn't see the cars, she could hear them, and on the opposite side were working factories.

She was half an hour from her destination, wherever the hell that was. She walked along a canal, water clogged with litter and foliage. The path at her feet was overgrown and although it could have made a nice dog walking or running route, she had a feeling it wasn't used too often by the general public.

She brushed passed a bush of mouldy, black leaves and it reminded her of Ria splayed out on the floor of her apartment, vines twining up her skin like some sick, parasitic plant. Now she was away from it, now she was here, outside in the sun and listening to birds and the sounds of normal life, she was questioning the whole experience.

She shouldn't have left her. She should have just called an ambulance—could still do that, now. But her feet kept on going, driven on by the urge to do something—anything.

Her heart was beating a mile a minute. She put a hand there, but took it away just as quickly, scared at how quick she could feel it against her palm. Was she having a panic attack? She didn't know what one of those felt like but she definitely felt on the brink of an all-out freakout.

She came to a fork in the path and the route guided her to the left, onto a rusty metal bridge, and she took a moment to lean against it and gaze into the dirty, rushing waters below. When her heart had calmed enough, she minimized her map app and brought up the photo of Ria. The picture was a bit blurry and the blackness looked more like smudged soot than anything else but there was no denying the change in her face. Ruth brought the phone closer to her, running her eyes over the ridges of Ria's face, the high cheekbones and unnaturally pink lips. How could something be so beautiful and so horrifying at the same time? When she felt a disturbing stirring between her legs, she straightened up from the bridge and continued on.

This path was even more choked and more disturbingly, every so often she'd see a sign poking out of the foliage, with *DANGER, Electric shock risk* printed on it. Was she even allowed to be here? Probably not, though she hadn't seen any no access signs—but neither had she seen any other people.

When the path forked again, she took a moment to consult her map before continuing to the right. It was barely a path and she hadn't moved a few meters forwards along it until she was stopped by a temporary fence. There was no away around it and even if there was, the only thing beyond it from what she could see, was a lake.

Sighing, Ruth backpedaled and took the left path. It veered around whatever woodland area she was in; the road was visible here and it offered her some comfort as she ducked under stray branches. A boundary fence sprang up on her right side and as she followed it, the most peculiar humming infused the air. Craning her head, she took in the powerlines running above her. Yeah, she really shouldn't be here. Yet she continued on because if she didn't, she'd have to return to the city, return to Ria…

The humming was freaky. It was probably her imagination, the staticky feeling running along her skin, the feeling that she'd be zapped by the power grid at any second. But whilst there was still some semblance of a path, she'd keep going.

She passed by a small cabin, spotting a man wearing an orange hi-vis jacket in the window. She ducked her head and sped up but couldn't ignore the knocking from the window as she passed. Stifling a sigh, she looked up at him, nodding in acquiescence at his elaborated hand motions as he pointed her back the way she'd come.

Well, she was stumped. She stuck her phone back into her pocket, stuffing her hands in them too. She'd have to go back to the apartment. The thought constricted her heart. She didn't think she could handle it if Ria still looked…like that. Even worse, what if she was dead? Ruth had been out here a while now, traipsing around, looking for god-knows-what. What kind of help did Ria *need* anyway?

God, she could go for a cigarette right now. The thought made her snort. She didn't even have her e-cig on her. She could feel her fingers itching for the comfort of it. They curled around her phone instead and she pulled it back out, calling Ria's mobile number on a whim.

No answer.

When she got back to the dirt road where the taxi had dropped her off, she spotted another path she hadn't given much notice to before. Though shadowed by overhanging branches, it was wide, the mouth of it obstructed with concrete blocks that she squeezed through after giving a cursory glance to a couple of factory workers eyeing her with interest.

They didn't stop her and soon she was out of sight. She opened her map app again. She'd give this whole thing one last go before going back to the flat.

The dirt path quickly dissolved into overgrown grass. Up ahead, in the distance, she could see a burnt out vehicle and in front of that, some kind of mini greenhouse and a washing line encumbered with clothes. Someone lived here?

Ruth flitted her eyes all around but she didn't spot anyone, not even as she got up close to the vehicle. She rounded it warily, nearly stopping in her tracks when the thin path suddenly opened up onto an avenue of caravans. There was loads of them, stacked right up close together, with more washing lines connecting the tops of them.

For all the evidence of life, she still couldn't *see* any. She only hoped this community was friendly. Looking at her map, she could see she was close to her destination, coming right on top of it, in fact.

As she continued on, a door to one of the caravans opened and a man stepped out. He was skinny and kind of dishevelled and he gave her a weird look before disappearing into the caravan opposite. She wasn't getting friendly vibes so far. Hunching down in her jacket, she increased her speed, eyes on the end of the line of caravans.

She thought she was home-free when something suddenly knocked her off her feet. She landed on the ground with a *thump*, hands still too tangled in her pockets to break her fall. She rolled onto her back to see who had pushed her, and came eye to eye with—well, she wasn't sure what, but it was bloody ugly. Small and brown and wrinkled. There were three of them, all leering at her from under heavily furrowed brows.

Freeing her hands, Ruth peddled backwards. Every

instinct screamed at her to get up and run but she was stuck there, mind too dazed to make sense of what she was seeing. They looked like some kind of CGI creatures but they were *real*, right in front of her, and getting closer. She held up a palm, instinctively warding them off. They didn't take too kindly to that, the corners of their mouths turning up in a sneer.

Ruth jumped to her feet. The things only came to her thighs and though her fear lessened, she still eyed them like she was confronting a couple of vicious dogs. She started backing away slowly, the hairs on her back raising at the sound of a caravan door shutting behind her.

She made a break for it. Turning, she tried to dive past the person there but they caught her by the arms. 'Oh no you don't.'

'Get the fuck off!' On instinct, she kicked out, knee connecting with the point between the man's legs. She looked up at his face and her heart jumped. *'Jed?'*

'Jesus, girl,' he gasped, hunched over.

In his pain, he'd let her go. She immediately jumped behind him, eyes on the creatures who still stood in an arc, watching.

'Can we eat her?' one asked, voice raspy.

'No, you fucking can't!' Jed waved his arm and the creatures jumped back and then, giving one last look at Ruth, waddled away.

'What are they?' Ruth breathed.

'Your standard bastard goblins, those.' He straightened up, a pained grimace still on his face. 'Carnivores, cannibals, a complete pain in my ass.'

'From your…stories?'

Jed nodded. 'I told you, kid—real.'

The goblins disappeared beneath a caravan and Ruth shuddered to think there might be a whole nest of the things under there. Suddenly remembering why she was here, she turned back to Jed and said, 'I think I need help.'

Ruth sat against the sofa of Jed's caravan. It formed an L-shape beneath the main window which was green with algae and looked straight out onto the window of the caravan next to it. That window had its curtains pulled tight.

Ruth took in the dim, small interior of the caravan.

'So this is where you live?'

'Not exactly,' Jed grunted, fiddling with a camping stove, a dented copper tea kettle sitting atop it. 'Sometimes.'

'Are you...?' She wasn't sure how to phrase it. She wasn't sure how any of this was happening. 'You're not—you're normal, aren't you?'

'You asking me if I'm one of those bastards?' Ruth nodded, accepting the cup of tea he held out to her. 'Naw, I'm as human as you.' He sat down beside her heavily then asked, 'Ruth, what the fuck are you doing here?'

She nodded towards the window. 'I think I have a sick one of them.'

'You think?' Jed ran a hand over his face, then over the dome of his bald, tattooed head. He sighed. 'So what kind of trouble have you found yourself in this time?'

Ruth looked away from his unamused eyes. 'It found me.' She paused, collecting her thoughts. 'I met her. At the pub I work at.'

'What does she look like? Was she in her human form?'

Ruth frowned. This was fucking absurd. 'Well, yeah,' she said. 'She looked normal. Acted normal.'

'You fucking her?' Ruth looked away, a blush rising in her cheeks as she nodded. 'So what's the issue here. She's sick, eh?'

Ruth nodded. 'Really sick. Not conscious. Well, barely.'

'Where is she? Somewhere she won't be found?'

'Yeah, she's in this apartment. I'm starting to think it's not hers though.'

'Anyone else in there with her?'

Ruth shook her head. 'Don't think so. I've never seen

anyone.' She straightened up, suddenly remembering the photo on her phone. 'I have a picture of her.' She found the image and shoved the phone into Jed's lap.

'Well,' he said, studying it, 'at least you're fucking one of the pretty ones.'

'She changed to that.' Ruth gestured at the phone. 'I watched it happen like right in front of me. Before that, she was normal looking.'

Jed nodded. 'She was glamoured.' He tapped the screen. 'That's her normal form.'

Ruth gave a thought to the goblins. Could they do that then? Disguise themselves to be pretty? It made her stomach roil, the thought that Ria could just as easily be one of those.

'Do you know why she's sick?' Jed handed her back her phone.

'No. She just kind of collapsed on me. Asked me to get help. Gave me the coordinates to this place.' She shrugged. 'So I came.'

Jed sighed. 'Well, we need to know what's wrong with her.' He nodded towards her. 'Finish yer tea. Then we'll get off.'

CHAPTER 19

'Well, looks like she's regained some of her strength.'

They stood looking down at Ria, who had, in the time that Ruth had been gone, managed to move to the sofa and reglamour herself. Beside the kitchen island was a pool of vomit.

Ruth remained rooted to the spot as Jed kneeled beside Ria, picking up one of her hands.

'What are you doing?' Ruth asked. She watched Jed prick Ria's finger, smearing the black jewel of blood onto a strip of paper.

'Seeing what's wrong with her. This place,' he sighed, 'it ain't so good for those lot.'

Ruth frowned. 'What even are they? Why are they here then?'

'Fairies, kid, I told yer. The fae, the fair folk, the little ones. As to why they're here—well, most are exiled. For crimes against their own kind. This one though,' Jed said musingly, 'I'm not so sure about.' He tapped the piece of paper restlessly against his thigh. 'How long have you been seeing her?'

'Not long. About a month. Bit more.' That crawly feeling was back. Ria might look normal now, but the image of her with those cheekbones and black leaves was forever branded behind her eyelids. And the thought that she was having sex with that. Ruth shuddered. 'God, this is all so messed up.'

Jed chuckled dryly. 'Happy fucking Halloween.' He glanced down at the paper and grunted. 'Poisoned. Not iron.'

'Poisoned?'

'Well, you've been hanging out with her. Can you think of anything she might have ingested?'

Ruth frowned. 'Like what? I haven't given anything to her.'

'Lotsa things make a fairy sick when ingested.' His eyes went to the ceiling and he pursed his lips as he thought. 'Clover, limes, ash, St John's wort—'

'Wait, St John's wort? That something I put in my smoothies.' She nodded at Ria. 'She's been having them.'

Jed sighed, standing up. 'Well, that oughta do it. Damn silly thing. Least we know what we're dealing with now.'

'So now what?'

'Go back. Get some medicine.'

'So she'll live?'

'Reckon so.' He peered around the apartment. 'I wanna look around this place when I get back.'

'Wait, I'm coming with you.'

Jed shook his head. 'No.'

'*Yeah*, I am. You're not making me stay here with—her. Plus, I have questions.' She huffed out a laugh. 'A fucking tonne of them.'

Jed looked her straight in the eye. 'This shit's dangerous.'

Ruth shrugged, folding her arms. 'So's what we do urbexing.'

Jed sighed. 'Alright,' he said reluctantly. He glared at her. 'You best be good at keeping secrets.'

Ruth snorted. 'Got no one to tell them to.'

☙ ❧

The taxi ride back was tense. Small talk wasn't Jed's thing and though the stuff Ruth wanted to ask him were far from small, she felt weird asking with the cabbie there in the front. So she sat there silently, amassing questions and thinking about the nature of the girl she was having sex with.

She thought back over the course of their short relationship, if you could even call it that. She remembered the blood on Ria's hands the night of the Halloween party— it *had* been black—and how Ria was always so vague and intense about everything. Apart from that though…Ruth slumped down, sighing. She was so fucking gullible. Gullible and clearly blind as shit.

When they approached the avenue of caravans again, Ruth tensed up. She couldn't see any of those god-awful goblin things but she kept her wits tight about her anyway. They went into Jed's caravan again and he pointed at the sofa for her to sit while he rooted around in some wicker basket on the table.

'If we're going to do this, I want you at least a bit protected,' he said, voice still gruff with disapproval.

'Protected from what?'

Jed gave her a look. 'You don't know what you're about to be messing with.'

Ruth spread out her arms. 'Then bloody tell me.' She watched as Jed took a seat beside her, his hands holding things which looked freshly plucked from a garden. 'What am I dealing with here?'

Jed sighed. 'These lot—they've always been here. Always. Probably before we were. I don't know the specifics. They're from somewhere below.'

'Like Hell?'

Jed huffed. 'Some of 'em. It's a place—physical but also kinda set apart. Hard to get there for folks like us.'

Ruth pulled her knees up, wrapping her arms around her as she listened, unable to dispel the sensation that she was a kid being told fairy tales. 'Have you been there?'

One of Jed's shoulders lifted in a shrug. 'Once or twice.'

'How do you get there?' At that question, Jed gave her a look. Ruth shook her head. 'Whatever. What are you doing around these things?'

'Some of us, not a lot, but a few, have what we call the Sight. Means we can see through a fairy's glamour. Means we can see them for what they really are.'

'How'd you get it?'

'Born with it. Some genetic thing, I reckon. Maybe I got some fairy blood in me from way back when.'

Ruth digested that. 'So we—humans—can mate with them?'

'Some of them. Rare though.'

'So you're like, friends with them?'

Jed snorted. 'Wouldn't say that. Just gives me a pass, I guess.'

'So what do you do with them?'

'Help. They're pretty much fucked here. And yeah, most of them of are bloody awful but I'm a sucker for those in need.' He looked pointedly at Ruth's side, where the scars from the accident he rescued her from were still visible.

Ruth gave a small smile. 'You melt.'

'Fuck off.' He opened his fist, revealing the plant matter. 'Let's get these on yer.'

Ruth sat up, letting her legs fall back to the floor. 'What is all that?'

Jed held up a clover. 'Makes you see what I see. Don't want any of 'em playing tricks on yer. That's kind of their whole thing.' He tucked the clover into a small pouch held on a string. Then he held up some berries. 'Rowan. Same thing.'

Ruth let Jed put the pouch over her neck and she touched it briefly before tucking it under her shirt. 'That's such basic stuff.'

'Yep. Effective though.' He slapped his palm against his thighs and stood up. 'Come on then. Let's go get this medicine.'

Ruth stood up too but only a second later, she was on her knees as a zap to her head so painful knocked her off her feet. *'Jed,'* she breathed.

Jed dropped to his knees beside her. 'What is it lass?'

'Hurts,' she bit out. She had her head in her hands, gripping fistfuls of her hair tightly as the front of it pulsed with a pain so sharp, she thought her skull might split open. But then, just as suddenly, the pain began to ebb, leaving in its place— 'Oh, my god. Oh my god, oh my god, oh my god!'

'What? Ruth, what the fuck's going on?'

Ruth looked up at him with wild eyes. 'She took my memories, Jed—*she took my memories.*'

Jed looked sympathetic. 'Ah. Yeah, they can do that.' He glanced over at the wicker basket. 'Those berries will be undoing that magic. Sorry, kid. I didn't think.'

Ruth shook her head viciously. 'No, you don't get it. I knew her. Ria. From before. We were together, like *properly* together. And then we broke up because she—well, whatever—and then she came back the other month wanting to…get back together, I guess, or make amends or something, but I said no so she fucking *took* my memories so I wouldn't know who she was. Fuck! All this time and she *knows* me.'

Jed took in air between his teeth. 'That's some fuckery there. But believe it or not, I've seen worse. A whole lot worse.'

Ruth shook her head again, vision blinded by tears. She could see it all, *feel* it all. It was all slamming into her brain and she couldn't catch her breath and her head was going to explode—

'Ruth, calm down will yer.'

But she couldn't because she was feeling it all over again. Every damn thing. Ruth dug her nails into the vinyl flooring, bracing herself against the tide. Their eyes first meeting, the excitement; the lust quickly coalescing into love—god, so much love; Ria's dark eyes pouring over her, promising her forever, promising her everything; all the furious, passionate fights; the sex following them; then the night it all fell apart…

Unable to bear it, Ruth gathered up that hurt and

corralled it into anger.

She pulled herself to her knees, releasing a breath through her nose. She knew she didn't feel things like a normal person. She either felt it all or she felt next to nothing. And right now, she was feeling *everything*.

'You ready to get this medicine?' Jed asked, squeezing her shoulder.

Ruth slowly shook her head. 'No. Let her suffer. Fucking bitch.'

Jed sighed. 'That's fair but I just ain't got it in me. You stay here then. I'll be back.'

'No.' Ruth got to her feet. 'I'm coming. I want to see more of these bastards.'

'On your own head,' Jed muttered, opening the caravan door for her to go through.

Jed steered her left which took them past the line of caravans and into a messy, overgrown clearing. In the distance, over the tops of trees, Ruth could make out the shape of an old Ferris wheel. Even at this distance, she could tell it was long abandoned.

'Where are we going?' she asked.

'To their lair.'

Ruth snorted. 'So ominous.'

'You're wrong to make light of this, lass.' He glanced at her. 'This might be a lot for you—seeing them. Some ain't pretty.'

'I'll be fine.' And she would be. The anger hadn't abated one bit and the way she was feeling, she could take on fucking anything.

'Is it true about the iron thing?' she asked, eyes on a rusted pole sticking out of the grass.

Jed cut his eyes her way. 'Why you asking?'

'Is it?'

'Yeah. Hurts 'em. Hurts 'em good.'

Ruth only nodded, saying no more, but the things running through her head...

They came up parallel with the Ferris wheel and Ruth

craned her head to look up at it, spotting a lone figure sitting in one of the swinging benches near the top. They were slumped over the restraint bar and Ruth saw what looked like ram horns on their head. She couldn't tell their gender from here but they had on an old-biddy type nightgown, the bottom of it billowing in the wind. It was the only thing about them that moved.

'They alright?' she asked quietly.

Jed glanced at the wheel. 'Don't look it, do they?'

They veered away from the wheel, approaching a dilapidated, office-style building. It's brown walls were probably once a sandy colour and most of the many square windows were smashed through. The only points of colour was the graffiti sprayed on the two front doors. Ruth tried to decipher the symbols. They didn't look like the sloppy tags that teens would scrawl; she wondered if they were fae writings.

'This it?'

'This is it. City of Rust, the locals call it.' He smiled without humour and opened the door for her.

The entry hall was dim, smelled of mildew and was just as cold as outside, if not colder with the breeze whipping down the corridor. Straight ahead of them was a precarious set of stairs and this was where Jed headed, Ruth trailing behind, keeping an eye out for glimpses of fairy things.

At the top of the stairs was another corridor, lined by shut doors along one side, and large windows on the other, most smashed through so that Ruth could see down into a centre courtyard.

There were beings in that courtyard. Ruth moved closer to the windows, looking down. The courtyard was all weeds and cracked concrete and there were old school-style tables ladened with foodstuffs, which these beings swarmed. Ruth didn't know where to look first. She saw some tiny goblin types, sitting atop each other's shoulders so they could reach the food; people who looked mostly human if not for the odd animal feature spouting from them—horns and strange ears and thin tails whipping back and forth. At the far end was a huge, round thing. It commandeered one end of the table, growling whenever the goblins weaved too close to it. It was so grotesque it reminded Ruth of a cancer tumour, only one with legs and arms. She saw it reach down and in one savage motion, rip a limb off a charred—

'Jed, it's eating a dog.'

'Yeah.'

Ruth grabbed his arm. 'A fucking *dog*, Jed.'

Jed whirled around, causing her to remove her hand in surprise. 'If you ain't got the stomach for this,' he growled, 'then you better tell me now.'

Ruth stared back, trying to smother the glimmer of fear and disgust. She patted around for that anger she'd been feeling before, picturing Ria's face, and drew it back around her like a comforting cloak. 'I'm good.'

Jed resumed walking and Ruth followed, though she kept her eyes on the courtyard, looking at what remained of the dog until the sense of revulsion subsided.

They had rounded almost all of the courtyard before Jed finally stopped outside a set of double doors. 'Stick close to me,' he muttered before pushing them open. Ruth craned her head, trying to peek over his shoulder.

The room beyond was dim because it was so large and most of the windows had tangled blinds crisscrossing over them. Despite not being able to see well, Ruth could sense all the bodies around her. Their shadows were wrong—too hulking, too skinny, too squat.

Ruth wished there was more light to see them by. And more air. The place stank. Not like sweat, not like the dankness of too many bodies crammed together in one space, but more like wet soil, though Ruth couldn't see mould on any of the walls.

'This way,' Jed barked when she strayed from his side. Ruth stiffened, fighting the urge to resist. She wanted to stalk to the left side of the room, right there in the corner, where she could have sworn she'd just seen a girl with wings.

As she hastened to catch up with Jed, a girl brushed her side. Ruth followed her with her eyes as she passed by and the girl looked back, giving her a pursed-lipped smile as if to say, *look at us, being where we shouldn't.* The girl was undoubtedly human, dressed in ripped mom jeans and an oversized jumper. Ruth kind of wanted to stop her and ask her things but Jed had already left through another set of doors and was glaring back at her.

As she caught up with him, she found herself wondering just how many humans knew of this other world, how many had this Sight that Jed had. Did the president of the world even know? He talked about aliens sometimes but not fairies. Did her own prime minister know, while the rest of population languished in ignorance?

It was a lot. Ruth would give anything to be in her flat right now, alone, preferably with a bottle of rum and enough quiet to sort through the sludge in her head.

But instead she was traipsing at the heels of someone she thought she knew, like some puppy, on a mission to gather medicine for a person she quite frankly now hated with all of her heart. Her chest tightened at that last bit. Okay, maybe it wasn't hate. Hurt? Betrayal? Something to figure out later at any rate.

Jed had stopped outside a door off the corridor. He gave her a look before opening it. This room was well-lit and Ruth immediately wished it wasn't. It was a hospital bay— had to be. There weren't beds along the walls but mats of what looked like hard-packed leaves and on those mats were sick fairies—very sick fairies. Most were unconscious, their faces pale, despite the hue of their skin. Ruth passed a male fairy the colour of green olives, another a shade lighter than red wine.

On her right, on the other side of Jed, a large male fairy pitched to one side of his mat and heaved onto the carpet. From his mouth gushed what looked like black caviar. Next to him, a creature with spikes protruding from her shoulders turned away and moaned, wrapping her arms around her head.

The one Ruth knew would stick with her most was the last mat on the bay, where a tiny, slip of a creature laid. Ruth bet she could circle her waist with both hands, and still have her fingers touch. Her skin was the most incredible pearlescent blue and though it shimmered beautifully in the weak sunlight, when her eyes captured Ruth's, she saw they were as hollow as empty graves—the eyes of someone who knew they were about to die.

'What's wrong with them all?' she asked quietly.

Jed shrugged, not bothering to look around. 'Lotsa things. This is a pretty poisonous place for them.'

Ruth glanced back at the blue girl, wondering what on earth she could have done to warrant exile, to warrant this kind of fate.

The next room they entered was smaller but lined with shelves and cabinets. Whilst the hall they passed through earlier smelled like mulchy earth, this was scented more like a spring garden. Along the shelves were bunches of drying herbs and wreaths of berries—not the ones hanging around her neck—and jars of dried stuff and vases of tincture liquids. There were other things too—more human things, like empty IV bags and syringes. Along the only windowsill in the room were vials of propagated plants, roots hanging into the water like tapeworms.

From behind Jed's back, Ruth tried to take it all in. This must be the medicine room. This was the help she was meant to get Ria.

Jed waved a hand at a woman in the far corner, garnering her attention. The woman turned and Ruth tried not to stare at the narrow tusks pulling down from her lips. Other than those, she looked mostly human.

'Got a poisoning,' Jed grunted. 'St John's wort.' He glanced at Ruth. 'Been in her system a while. She ain't local so will need a kit to go.'

The woman frowned. 'Hope it isn't urgent. We haven't got anything to hand.'

Jed gestured at the room, encompassing its contents. 'How?'

'I'm sorry but—St John's wort.' The woman shook her head. 'Most aren't stupid enough.'

Ruth felt an unwelcome stab of guilt. She was the one who'd been poisoning Ria all these weeks. She hadn't known, but still. She pushed it down, letting the anger swallow it up like a bath of acid.

She looked over the room again as movement caught her eyes. A tiny man walked out from behind the woman, his gait moving side to side so it was more like a waddle. Ruth tensed. He wasn't one of those goblins, but it was close enough. He pulled a stepladder over to another place in front of the shelves and stepped up it, sighing heavily as he reached out to pluck one of the jars. He turned his head and barked something Ruth couldn't make out and she caught an answering wave. Sitting on a chair in the far corner beside the shelves was a man—at least Ruth thought he was a man. He was androgynous, pretty-faced and dressed in long clothes the colour of silver. He crunched on an apple, gaze on the tiny man who was still warbling things at him. Ruth found herself thinking he'd make a great drag queen.

When his eyes cut to hers, she looked away.

She felt a bit invisible in the room, watching Jed talk with the tusked woman. As she shifted on her feet, looking from those tusks, to the strange stuff all over the shelves, to the tiny fae creature on the ladder, she felt a wave of derealisation so strong, she had to squeeze her fists together to ground herself.

God, she wasn't cut out for this shit.

'I've not seen you around here before.'

Ruth started at the smooth voice in her ear. The pretty man stood beside her, twirling an apple core and smiling at her with a benign, neutral smile.

Ruth opened her mouth to reply that she was new here, but that sounded like something of a weakness, so she said nothing. She glanced back to Jed but he was busy with the tusked woman.

'Do you have a sick friend?' the fairy continued.

This time Ruth felt rude ignoring him so she replied, 'Kind of.'

He uttered a quiet 'ah', seemingly sympathetic. They watched Jed for a few moments before he turned to her fully. 'I'm Nevarold—Nevar, if you wish.'

He held out a hand and Ruth looked at it warily, as if his touch alone could take away her memories, or turn her into a toad, or bind her to him forever. Whatever fairies were supposed to do. And maybe it could, for all Ruth knew.

Smile turning wry, Nevar retracted his hand.

'I'm Ruth,' she said hastily, hoping to overturn the sudden awkwardness.

Nevar's smile brightened. He nodded towards Jed. 'It will take them some time to compose the bag. I will be happy to entertain you until then.'

Ruth didn't know what that meant. She flicked her gaze to Jed who had overheard the offer. He waved her off without concern. 'I'll get you,' he said.

Shrugging internally, Ruth followed Nevar into a small room at the back of the medicine room. It was more of a cupboard than anything, but there were two chairs tucked under a small table, an empty bottle atop it. The faint smell of wine told her what the bottle had once contained.

'Sit,' Nevar said brightly.

Ruth did, her eyes raking over him as he took the seat opposite. How could he not be human? He talked like one, looked like one—albeit a beautiful one with weird clothes. What about them was different? Was it their blood, their genes? Were they from the same genetic tree as humans, only shot off it a little earlier or a little later? How had they stayed hidden all this time, peeking up in only stories and lore? And their magic—how did she begin to make sense of that?

'My apologies for not having a drink to off you,' Nevar said, looking genuinely aggrieved as he set the empty wine bottle on the floor.

'It's cool.'

'A game!' Nevar swept a hand in front of the items on the table and Ruth glanced at them, identifying for the first time what looked like a small game board replete with pieces. Nevar began resetting the pieces. They glowed all kind of colours in the light of the naked bulb above them and Ruth was reminded of moonstone.

He set the pieces slowly, carefully, explaining how to play as he did. His voice was lovely, lightly accented and lilting. If she was speaking to anyone else, she would think they were putting it on.

It turned out the game was kind of like chess, only with less pieces and a few extra rules thrown in. When Nevar had set the board up, he gestured at her to take the first turn.

She reached out then hesitated. 'What happens if one of us wins?' Nevar tilted his head. 'I mean, what are the stakes?' She sat back, waiting. Fairies liked that kind of thing, didn't they? Bargains, games. Or was that just made up stuff? She was having a difficult time separating myth from reality right now.

'A human, so quick to bargain. What a treat.' Nevar sat back too. 'The stakes, if you *insist*.' He pursed his lips. 'If *I* win…' He paused for a moment, glancing at the glass bottle on the floor. 'If I win, you will gift me a bottle of your most favoured wine, and if *you* win—'

'You have to answer any question I have.'

One silver-blonde eyebrow rose at that but Nevar nodded, nevertheless. 'We have a deal, human.' He nodded at her to take her turn again.

Ruth slowly waggled her fingers over the board as she thought. She'd never actually played chess before—no one had ever taught her—so she was pretty out of her depth here. And to be honest, she couldn't give a toss about the game. If Nevar wouldn't answer her questions, Jed would.

She reached out and carelessly pushed forward one of her smallest pieces. Nevar inclined his head at her choice and moved one of his. It went like that for a few minutes until finally Nevar reached out and toppled her queen-piece. Ruth's shoulders slumped.

'Best of three?' Nevar said, rightening the pieces.

They played again and by some miracle, Ruth managed to beat him. She tipped over his queen-piece gently, not feeling like she'd earned the clack of it hitting the board.

As Nevar reset the board for a third time, she spared a glanced towards the door, wishing Jed would hurry up.

Nevar took his first turn and stifling a sigh, Ruth did too, dropping the piece onto its square with a careless thunk. Nevar immediately slid one of his pieces forward, eyes keen on the board as she reached out for her turn.

As soon as she had, Nevar flicked out his hand and toppled over his queen-piece, leaning back in his chair with a small smile.

'What?' Ruth flittered her eyes over the board, trying to figure out how she won so easily. 'You let me win,' she accused.

Nevar smiled and offered her a shrug. 'It seems I am keen to talk to you. What is it you'd like to know, earthling?'

Ruth reached out and grasped the toppled piece, warming the cool crystal in her hand as she thought.

'Why are you here?' she began with. 'What was your crime?'

'Crime?'

Ruth replaced the piece back onto the board. She knew she was fidgeting and tried to stop. 'Aren't you exiled?'

Nevar chuckled quietly. 'We do not *have* to be exiled to be here.'

'Then why?'

Nevar pursed his lips. 'I like it here,' he said simply. He grinned at Ruth's subsequent frown. 'You are wondering what there is to like. I enjoy your cultures. There are so many of them. I may not understand them but that in itself makes them interesting.'

'Do you not have 'culture' where you're from?'

'Not in the same way. Our way of life is more…frivolous. Frivolity does not breed culture.'

'That sounds like a culture to me.'

'Perhaps. But to tell the truth, it bores me. Immensely.' He went on, 'You humans—you are also free.'

Ruth was dubious. 'Are we?'

'In a way. Maybe it's not a freedom which you can see. One never sees the treasures of one's own culture.'

Ruth wasn't sure what treasures lay here in shitty Manchester but frankly she didn't really care. Her next question interested her more. 'What can you do?' she asked. 'Like, what magic?'

Nevar's eyes dropped to the protection pouch which had fallen from her shirt. 'Rid yourself of that and I can show you, if you'd like?'

Ruth grasped the pouch, not at all liking the teasing smile on his lips. 'Nice try.' The smile turned into a grin. 'Can you take away memories?'

'Now, why would I want to do that?'

'Can you?'

Nevar inclined his head. 'If I so pleased.' Ruth looked away, feeling his keen gaze on her, studying her. 'I am not the first fae you've encountered,' he said. A statement, not a question. Ruth shook her head. 'You have been burned.' He leaned towards her. 'And you *anger*.'

Ruth looked back up at him. There was a curious look in his eyes. Following an impulse, she took out her phone, brought up the picture of Ria and tossed in onto the table in front of him. 'Do you know her?'

Nevar looked down at the picture, eyebrows immediately raising. 'What did you do to her?'

'Nothing. Do you know her?'

Slowly, Nevar nodded. 'Not personally, but she is well known. Very well known. Heiress to the other court, in fact.'

'What do you mean—court?'

'The unseelie court.' Nevar cocked his head. 'You truly are new to all of this, aren't you?'

'I think…' Ruth furrowed her brows. 'I think I've heard of that in stories. There's two isn't there? Two courts?' Nevar nodded. 'One bad, one good.'

Nevar laughed. 'How simplified. But if it helps you to understand.' He glanced back down at the phone, the screen now black. He suddenly seemed troubled. 'It is she who you are getting medicine for?' Ruth nodded. 'You cannot allow her to die, no matter the ways in which she harmed you. They would seek vengeance and seek it hard. Do you understand?'

Ruth nodded. She did, clearly. Basically, she would be fucked if Ria died. But god, did she want her own revenge on that lying, memory-erasing bi—

'Having said that,' Nevar said, relaxed again, 'it takes much to kill a fairy.' He winked at her and Ruth couldn't help but smile back. It was like he had read her thoughts.

'Ruth.' Jed stood in the open door. He gestured with his head for her to follow.

Ruth rose, glancing back to Nevar who remained seated.

'Nice to meet you, Ruth,' he said. Ruth smiled briefly, leaving him sitting in the little room.

'You got the medicine?' she asked Jed.

'Yup. Let's get it back to your fairy.'

CHAPTER 20

They trudged back to the woodland edge where Ruth stopped to call a taxi.

'My phone's dead,' she said, pressing the home button a number of times before trying the on switch.

Beside her, Jed checked his own phone then sighed. 'That happens sometimes. It's part of their magic. Doesn't really belong up here so it fucks with things sometimes. God, I hope it's still today.'

Ruth jammed her phone back into her pocket. 'What do you mean?'

'Told yer—fucks with things. Including time.'

Ruth stared at him. 'As in more time might have passed?'

'Relax. I'm only talking a few hours—couple days at most.'

Ruth gritted her teeth in frustration. It seemed weird to be thinking about work after everything today, but here she was, worrying that Sheila might be pissed at her for missing a shift.

'How do we get back?'

'Let's walk for a bit. Phones might come on yet.'

They found the main road and followed it, periodically checking their phones for signs of life.

'Mine's on,' Jed finally said, bringing up the number of a taxi service.

Ruth checked hers—still off. She didn't dare ask him what day it was.

When they got back to the apartment, Ruth made Jed go in before her, suddenly overcome with dread.

'Still alive,' he assured her. 'Right, how we gonna do this then?' He gestured to the kitchen island. 'Grab that chair there, will yer.'

Ruth pulled the chair over and Jed placed it atop a side table next the sofa where Ria still lay. Ruth stepped up to her, chest immediately seizing. God, it was her. The girl who'd broken her heart a year and a half ago, the girl she'd loved so *fucking* much that she thought she might die when she found her kissing that other girl—had wanted to die, even. That want didn't seem too far from the surface all of a sudden.

'Now ain't the time, lass.'

Ruth swiped a hand over a wet cheek and shook her head. 'I'm fine.' Digging her nails into her fisted palms, she sniffled, watching as Jed set up the IV bag on the chair and fiddled with the syringe. With the ease of someone who had done this before, he inserted it into Ria's forearm and taped it steady.

With a sigh, he straightened. 'That oughta do it.' Hands on hips, he surveyed the apartment. 'Time to have a look around then.'

As he walked around, opening cupboards and looking through drawers, Ruth asked him, 'What are you looking for?'

'Some sign of the bastard who lived here before.'

He walked into the bedroom and Ruth followed, unable to help glancing at the bed and thinking of all the things she and Ria had done in it. It was there, in that bed, that they'd first said *I love you.*

She was startled by Jed's gruff cry, 'Ah, yer bastard!'

She rushed over to the wardrobe, where her stomach immediately dropped. 'What? Oh my god—who is that?'

There was a man sitting amidst the coat rack, dressed in a crumpled suit, legs lying akimbo. Even from the doorway, Ruth could smell the odour of piss wafting up from him.

Jed knelt in front of him grimly. 'The poor sod who lives here, I'd say.'

Ruth stepped closer. The man was making noises—muted, keening sounds and his face was shiny with sweat. 'What's wrong with him?'

'Glamoured into a stupor. Your fairy did this. Probably ain't the first time either.'

'God, they're fucking evil.' The man was freaking her out, the way his teeth were bared in a grimace, his eyes roaming sightlessly. 'Will he be alright?'

'Yeah.' Jed stood. 'Soon as she wakes up, we'll get her to take it off him.'

As soon as she wakes up. Ruth's heart sped up. She could barely deal with all this with her unconscious. She needed more time to prepare herself.

Back in the living room, the IV bag bubbled away. Was it her imagination, or did Ria have more colour in her cheeks?

'How long will it take her to—to wake up?'

'Who fucking knows,' Jed muttered, checking the IV bag.

Outside, the balcony showed that the sun was setting, turning the undersides of clouds pink. It reminded Ruth of the night she met Ria and her stomach dropped and the grief was suddenly so strong, she almost forgot how to breath.

She cheated on you. She cheated on you and then when life was getting back to okay, she came and took your memories and fucked it all up for a second time. Ruth drew in a long breath, scrabbling around for that anger again. When she found it, she turned to Jed.

'I'll stay with her,' she said. 'You can go.' Jed hesitated. 'Seriously. I'll be fine.'

'Will you?'

Ruth shrugged. Probably not but she didn't want Jed privy to that particular fall out. 'It's just, we've got—shit to sort out. Kinda don't want an audience.'

'Alright. Just you be careful. These lot—you don't want to anger them. Those grudges don't dissolve so easily.'

'Jed, just go,' she finally snapped, her anger at Ria bubbling over. 'I'm not a fucking kid!'

Jed raised his hands. 'Alright. Alright.' He looked in the direction of the bedroom. 'Don't forget you've got that to deal with too.'

Ruth nodded and Jed made to leave the apartment.

'By the way,' Jed stuck his head back through the door, 'it's Friday, not Wednesday. We've been gone two days.' Then he was gone.

Ruth swore, pulling out her phone and uselessly poking at its buttons. She glanced at Ria. She owned a phone so there must be a charger around somewhere.

She found it in the bedroom. She sat down on the bed and plugged it in, waiting none too patiently for it to power up. 'Come on.' At first there was a no service warning as everything loaded and then the date flashed up. Friday. Her birthday—Halloween—was two days ago. 'What the actual hell?'

Her heart sped up as a number of missed call notifications pinged at her. Most were from Sheila but there were also a few from a number she didn't recognise. She tried that one first, not in the mood right now to have her ear chewed off.

'Hi there, Miss Mason,' the unknown voice said, *'This is Doctor Kayani calling from the Manchester Royal Infirmary. You're listed as an emergency contact number for a Ms Sheila Brown…'*

Ruth's blood ran cold. She gripped her phone tighter, eyes unfocussing as she listened to the voicemail. When it had finished, her hands were shaking.

Sheila—taken ill. Sheila—unconscious. Sheila who had needed her two fucking days ago.

Ruth got to her feet. She had to get to the hospital but if she took her phone now, there was no way the battery would last in case Ria—oh, fuck Ria. This was all her fucking fault anyway. All of it.

The anger was firmly back in place but so was panic and it clouded her mind. She closed her eyes and stood for a moment, making an actionable list in her mind. First—call a taxi. Get to Sheila. Ria could wait. Ruth doubted she would wake any time soon anyway. She had other priorities.

But as she got to the front door, she paused. But what if Ria did wake? Ruth wouldn't put it past her to do a runner, to piss off back to wherever she'd come from. Especially since this wasn't actually her apartment. And she couldn't have that. She needed answers, she needed the closure she'd never got before.

Letting out an impatient breath, Ruth walked back to the bedroom. She wasn't sure what she was looking for, just something that would secure Ria and render her incapable of escape. She considered the cord of the dressing gown pegged to the door but it probably wouldn't be enough to hold her.

Hesitantly, she ducked into the wardrobe, purposefully not meeting the man's eyes. His noises escalated when he saw her and she whispered a *sorry* as she rifled through his things. There wasn't much in here besides clothes but at the far end were a couple of storage boxes which she pulled towards her. Opening one, she grimaced awkwardly at its contents. Really not what she wanted to see. But as she began to close the lid, a flash of metal caught her eyes. Handcuffs. Ruth let out a disbelieving huff and pulled them out, careful not to graze the rest of the stuff in the box. She glanced at the man, hoping he wouldn't remember this, before placing the box back on the shelf and returning to the living room.

Carefully, she pulled the chair down from the side table, trying not to jostle the IV bag. Then, reluctantly, she took Ria's arms and pulled them above her before securing the cuffs to her wrists, making sure they were looped around the chair first.

Ruth stood back. There. She wouldn't be able to escape now, not without that bloody chair attached to her.

Without another glance back, she hurried from the flat.

CHAPTER 21

Two hours later, Ruth stood at the door to the flat again, staring without seeing the number drilled into the door. 605—also the last three digits of the number to Sheila's cancer ward. Ruth swallowed, pushing down for the thousandth time the tears threatening to break from her, and finally unlocked the door.

A quick glance showed that Ria was still unconscious, though the tilt to her head showed that she might have awakened at some point.

God, Ruth was exhausted, and hungry, but there was an emptiness inside her that she didn't think either sleep or food would fill.

Without thought, she crossed to the fridge, taking from it a small pot of pesto pasta. As she rooted around for a fork, her eyes caught sight of a bottle of vodka on the shelf above. She reached out and plucked it.

She crossed to the balcony. It was dark out now, though not particularly late yet. Setting the bottle on the small table, she flipped the lid of the pasta pot and began to eat, blinking at the city lights before her. Despite her tiredness, she was probably going to be pulling an all-nighter. The thought of sleeping whilst that guy was in the wardrobe wasn't appealing. Plus, she wanted to be there when Ria woke up. After all, it was her fault that Sheila…

Ruth closed her eyes, biting her lip hard until it stopped trembling. Sheila. Bloody woman. Why hadn't she told her about the lung cancer? Ruth's chest hitched. Had she ever planned to tell her or was she not even worth telling? God, she had looked so ill in that bed. Well, she was—dying, even. Ruth shook her head and sniffed hard, shovelling in another forkful of pasta. It was just fucking impossible. Sheila couldn't die, it wasn't in her nature to just *give up*.

Especially not yet. Ruth needed her.

A sob burst from her and Ruth dropped the pot of pasta to the table, covering her mouth with a hand. *Oh god Sheila, please no.* Trying to calm her breathing, she pulled close the bottle of vodka and uncapped it, screwing her face up at the burn of it in her mouth. She took a few mouthfuls until the burning subsided and a warmth began travelling through her instead.

She would never get over the guilt of not being there when Sheila had been taken to hospital. She'd finally listened to the rest of the voicemails and the last one from Sheila felt like a stab to the heart. She had sounded scared. She had been conscious when first admitted and now she was probably never going to wake up again.

Fucking Ria. This was all her damn shitty fault.

Ruth stood up, taking the bottle over to the balcony rail and leaning against it. It was a cold night but she knew the drink would keep her warm just as good as any coat. For the first time since finding out about Sheila, she let herself think of what Ria had done. She remembered it—the moment her memories were taken. Her shock at seeing Ria again after so long, the anger. How she had forced her to break up with Molly. Ruth closed her eyes. Poor Molly. Ruth had actually liked her.

As usual, her sadness just as quickly turned to anger. How dare she. How fucking *dare* she. She honestly couldn't think of anything more immoral than pressing you way into someone's mind and twisting things inside for the pure benefit of yourself—without consent, without the other person's knowledge. How was that any different from rape? It wasn't.

She thought she could still feel Ria inside her head now, like she'd left dirty fingerprints in her mind, prints that would never be washed away. She took the glass bottle and knocked it against her forehead—once, twice—just enough that she could feel the pain of it through the warm numbness of the drink.

She tossed her mind back two years ago, when she'd first met Ria at the festival and commenced the happiest six months of her life, where everything flowed and she felt loved for the first time ever. There had been fights, sure— they were both hot-headed people and sometimes Ria could be more possessive than protective, but despite those times, things between them had been amazing and Ruth had been convinced that she had found—well, the *one*.

Ruth snorted. *Idiot. You bloody idiot.*

She fast-forwarded. She was at a Halloween party, drunk and dancing and happy, just before turning to see Ria sucking the face off another girl. She could still feel the acid in her stomach, how the hurt and anger had sobered her up instantly. The fight they'd had on the street when Ruth had left to go home, how she'd cursed Ria to high heavens, never wanting to see her again. And she hadn't, not until a month or so ago.

Ruth sniffed. God, how could it still make her cry?

It had fucked her up pretty good, marking the start of her depression and meds and smoothies and all of that shit.

A yawn wracked through her and she leaned heavily against the railing, eyes falling to the dark grass below. It made her waver for a moment. The gardens reminded her of a dark pit, swallowing any light. She wondered how it would feel to fall into that pit. Had wondered that many, many times since Ria had trampled her heart. It wouldn't take much, just a foot up on the rail, a slight tilt over the edge and the wind would come to aid her, giving her that final push.

But Ruth laughed aloud because, despite her macabre thoughts, despite the fucked-up-ness of her life right now, a strange thrumming was pulsing through her and she had never felt more *alive*, because fairies were fucking real!

A whole damn world of them. It made her think—what else, what else? It made her want to live and find out.

Dizzily, she thunked the bottle down on the table and let out a quick, steadying breath, scrubbing the drying tears from her cheeks. Giving one last look to the city which suddenly seemed more colourful, more bright, she turned away.

When she went back inside, Ria was awake.

CHAPTER 22

They looked at each other for a moment until Ria's eyes fell shut again. She might be awake but she was still clearly unwell. She opened her mouth and mumbled something, something that Ruth didn't catch.

She stepped towards the sofa. 'What?'

'I said—the handcuffs.' A shuddering breath. 'Take them off.'

Ruth snorted. 'Don't think so.'

'They're hurting me.'

Ruth glanced at her wrists. 'I didn't put them on that tight.'

Ria gave a weak, frustrated sigh. 'No. The iron. It hurts.'

'But they're not made from iron. They're steel.'

'Steel is made from iron!' Ria closed her eyes, taking in another shuddering breath. 'You stupid—'

'Yeah, wow. Great way to treat the person that's just saved you.'

'And made me sick in the first place.'

Ruth tilted her head. 'How do you know?'

Ria glanced at the IV bag. 'This concoction. It is for a certain poison.'

Ruth nodded, vanquishing any feeling of guilt. Ria deserved this. Ria deserved to suffer for all she had done. 'My smoothies.'

Ria fell still and looked at her closely. 'You have been crying.'

'Don't change the subject.'

Ria regarded her from under heavy lids. 'Did you know? Is that why you poisoned me?'

'Know?' Ruth raised both her eyebrows. 'That you aren't human? No, I didn't bloody know that.' She ran a withering glance over Ria. 'Poisoning's probably more your speed. Call this karma.'

Silence lapsed as they regarded each other again until Ria finally said, 'You are angry.'

Ruth shook her head. 'You have no idea.' She walked over to the sofa and perched on its edge, close to Ria, taking a certain satisfaction in her lying there, unable to escape. 'You took my memories.' The rage seized her again. 'Do you know,' she said, voice shallow, barely controlled, 'how much of a violation that is?' Ruth studied Ria's face, trying to see even a hint of sorrow, but there was none. She snorted. 'You're a fucking psychopath.' She felt tears prick her eyes, but she forbade them to fall. 'Why did you do it?'

'To give us a second chance. To…right the wrongs.'

'Well you fucked that up, didn't you? And you can't just—Ria, I didn't *want* you. I was with someone else for fuck's sake!'

'And were you as happy with her as you were with me?' Ruth stared at her, unable to respond. Ria relaxed back, as if that was enough of an answer.

'You cheated on me.'

Ria shook her head. 'No.'

'Ria, I was there!'

'*No*,' Ria said again. She took in a slow breath. Ruth could tell she was struggling. 'Listen to me, listen well. That girl—she was not human. She was of my kind, glamoured. She forced me. It was either that or she killed you.'

'Killed me?'

Ria nodded. 'To get back at me—my father. She's exiled. I told her she couldn't go back, not ever, and that angered her. She was trying to punish me.'

Ruth frowned, looking away. That was a bit too much

and a big part of her was unwilling to forgive Ria for that particular betrayal, no matter what.

'You never told me.'

'No, Ruth. You would have thought me mad. Would you have believed me?'

Ruth shook her head slowly. 'Probably not.'

'So now you see. I did not wish to betray you. I would never want that.'

'And yet you did,' Ruth laughed, throwing her hands up for emphasis. 'By taking my memories! By pretending you didn't know me, *dating* me like we were strangers. That's so fucked! You've been lying to me, knowing this whole time that I didn't want to be with you but you forced me anyway. And now—' She stopped, unable to speak over the sudden lump in her throat. She was thinking about Sheila, the most unforgivable thing about all of this. She sniffed. 'I'm so mad at you.'

'It is justified.'

'No, Ria. I want to fucking *kill you*.'

'Do it then.' Risarial closed her eyes. 'It would be no less than what I deserve.'

'No.' Ruth shook her head. 'No, no, no—you do not get to play the victim here. Fuck you, Ria.'

'Risarial.'

'What?'

'My name. It's Risarial.'

Ruth shook her head. 'More lies.' She ran the name over in her mind but daren't repeat it aloud in case she messed up. 'Someone said you're an heiress. To some court. Is that true?'

'It's true.'

'What does that mean exactly?'

'Do you wish to know about my world?'

Did she? She wasn't sure she liked what she'd seen of it so far. She shook her head. 'Not at the minute. I'm not done being angry.' A quick smile crossed Ria's face. Ruth frowned. 'What?'

'You,' Ria answered quietly. 'Beautiful, beautiful human.'

It was Ruth's turn to snort. 'Yeah, okay. You really gonna make me believe that you actually loved me?'

'I did,' Ria whispered. 'Heavens, I did—I *do*.'

'Well sorry, I don't believe it.'

'Ruth, let me go—please. It *hurts*.'

'Good. Because it's still nowhere close to how I'm feeling right now. Not even a little bit close.' But even as she said that, she felt a stirring of guilt because, god, Ria looked so miserable laying there, and there was a shininess in her eyes that Ruth thought might be tears. Before she could dwell on that too much, she stood up. 'Take it off.'

'What?'

'Take it off—your—your glamour.' She couldn't bear another moment looking at Ria like this, like the girl she loved. It hurt too bloody much. She needed to see the monster beneath.

'No.'

'Do it!'

But Ria still refused so Ruth turned away instead, towards the window. It was getting on in the night. She probably shouldn't be shouting her head off. Exhaustion rolled over her and she closed her eyes, swaying on her feet.

'Well I must admit, this has been the most interesting birthday I've had in years,' she muttered.

'Your exhibition—how did it go?'

'Yeah, we're not doing that.' Ruth turned back to her and pointed at the bedroom. 'You need to sort that man out. Why did you do that to him?'

'I needed a place to stay.'

'Oh, so you forced him too? Are you all like that? All you fairies? Fucked in the head.'

'We are different to humans.'

'Then why were you with me? Why mess with some shitty little human?'

Ria's eyes softened and Ruth bristled. 'You are so much more than that,' she whispered.

152

'Is it common to—to—'

'Not common. But not unheard of.' Ria closed her eyes, sighing. 'The heart wants who it wants.'

'I want you to leave me alone.' Ruth glanced at the IV bag. It was almost empty. 'After this. And after you've helped that guy. I want you to piss off back where you came from and I literally never want to see you again. I mean it this time. Okay?'

For the first time, Ria's mask slipped and Ruth was almost shocked at the pain in her eyes.

'As you wish.'

CHAPTER 23

Sobbing from the cupboard woke Ruth up the next morning. She'd slept in the bed in the end, falling across it fully clothed mere hours ago. Her dreams had been almost feverish. She dreamed that Jed had turned into one of those goblins, his bald head too large on his new shoulders; she dreamed that that troll thing had decided Ruth would be a tastier snack than blackened dog; she dreamed of her and Ria having sex on the sofa, the IV tubing tied tight around them, binding them to each other.

Groaning, Ruth rolled out of the bed. On the sofa, Ria was awake, biting her lip, and as soon as she saw Ruth, she looked at her beseechingly. Knowing what she wanted, Ruth crossed to her and unlocked the cuffs.

As soon as she had, Ria cried out, cradling her arms to her chest, and Ruth was a little startled at the shiny red welts on her wrists. She didn't think it had been affecting her that much. Reaching out, she pulled the syringe from her and flung the tubing away.

'Go sort that guy out. Now.'

Shakily, Ria got to her feet and Ruth watched her disappear into the bedroom. Her stomach rumbled loudly and she put a hand to it. She was so hungry she could puke, and that was kind of making her not want to eat at all. The half-eaten pot of pasta was still sitting out on the balcony but it had rained in the night and it was just a soggy green mess now. Ruth took a banana from the fruit bowl, spotted with ripeness.

She watched the bedroom door. She kind of wanted to go in and see how Ria did it—watch her magic in real time. But she stayed rooted to the spot, chewing on the overly soft banana. A few minutes later, Ria returned.

'Done it?' Ruth asked. Ria nodded once, eyes not meeting hers. 'Do you...' She glanced at the fruit bowl. 'Do you need something to eat?'

Ria shook her head, lowering herself back down to the sofa. She'd changed out of the black dress and into jeans and an oversized jumper most likely belonging to the man in the wardrobe. God, she looked bad. Pale and drawn. Ruth tried to feel happy about it, but she struggled. In the light of a new day, she felt more hurt than angry.

'You know, I really fucking loved you,' Ruth said. 'The first time.'

'I know,' Ria whispered.

Ruth flung the banana skin away. 'Oh well.'

'Ruth.' When Ruth met her eyes, she said, 'I am in your debt. For saving me.'

Ruth shrugged. 'Don't worry about it.'

'No. I must reward you.' Her eyes bored into Ruth's. 'Anything you want.'

Ruth stared into her eyes. Anything? That was kind of loaded. She chewed on it for a while before coming to the conclusion that Ria had nothing she wanted. Nothing, except—

'Just don't come near me again. Ever. And Ria,' she turned towards the sofa, 'never, ever take my fucking memories away again.'

Hesitantly, so slowly Ruth thought she might decline, Ria nodded. 'It is done.'

'Good.' Ruth looked away. 'Probably time you fucked off now.'

Ruth heard Ria stand up, sway there for a second, before taking slow steps forward. She expected Ria to leave straight away but those steps were moving away from the door, and closer to her. She tensed, refusing to look behind her. Ria came to a stop at her shoulder and Ruth felt the heat of her. She wondered if Ria was still feverish, felt the urge to turn and touch her.

When she heard a soft *forgive me*, she tried to turn around but Ria had her gripped around the forehead, holding her immobile. She uttered something, something quick, something inhuman, and then those hands fell away. When Ruth finally managed to turn, Ria was gone.

She sat there for a disbelieving minute. Those words— she recognised them as the same ones Ria had whispered when she'd taken her memories the first time. Had she just tried to— 'Fuck!' Ruth kicked the kitchen island, the resulting bang drawing a gasp out from behind her.

The man stood in the bedroom doorway, staring at her wide-eyed. 'Are you—'

Ruth shook her head. 'I'm human. Sorry, I'll piss off in a sec. Just…getting my bearings.'

The man looked at the door, where Ria had just departed. 'I'm going to have to move,' he said brokenly. 'I'm going to have to go where she can't find me again. I can't go through—' His voice cracked.

'I don't think she'll be back.' The man sniffed and despite her renewed rage, Ruth felt awful for him. His trauma was evident. She reached for the necklace around her neck, took out the clover, putting it into her own pocket before she handed it to him. 'Here. Put it on. It'll stop them from doing their magic crap on you. Just in case.'

The man wasted no time in putting it over his head and then he stood there, stroking his thumb over the pouch reverently.

Ruth stood up. 'I'm gonna go. Sorry for…being here. And sorry for—her.'

The man nodded quickly, not looking at her and seeming like he wanted to forget the whole thing. Ruth could understand that. Picking up her phone from the kitchen island, she put on her boots and left the apartment for the last time.

CHAPTER 24

The moon was full. Risarial waited in the garden of the large white house, made whiter still by the globe above. She angled her head towards it, letting the coldness of it chill her even more. When it peeked behind a cloud, she looked back at the house. This was the one they'd told her to come to, this was the one where *she* resided. It was a prestigious building, long abandoned by its human owners—the walls crusted with dead trailing plants, gardens left to grow wild—but still held the air of affluence. The redcap had moved up in the world.

Movement above—a brownie up on a balcony giving her the signal. Risarial pushed away from the garden wall she leaned against, offering the brownie a nod. In the darkness, she stalked to the door, ascending its steps and pushing her way inside. The door squealed loudly but she didn't care. Inside was lit only by fat candles, catching on the dust-coated walls, matching the orange of her eyes—the only thing about her that still burned bright.

A horned head peeked around the corridor and looked at her. She looked back until it disappeared. No one would challenge her here. Tonight, she was untouchable.

She came to a closed door where a bogart stood. He took a step back as she approached but gestured to the door, nodding his boxy head. She took a deep breath, closing her fists and feeling the magic thrum through them. It had taken a few weeks, licking her wounds back at the court, for her to regain her strength following the poisoning. As for the wounds on her heart—it would take a few eternities or more for those to close. She only hoped tonight would help with that.

'Are they alone?' she asked.

The brownie twisted their gnarly hands together. 'You won't find any dissension in there, my lady.'

Good enough. She pushed open the door, lashing out a vine from her right palm and snuffing the candles in the room. The only light now was that of her eyes.

She smelled the blood of the redcap before she saw her. As she approached, other beings slinked away from her quarry, gathering behind her. She used their support, however bought, to further bolster her.

She heard the redcap sniff, sourcing the scent of her. 'Who's that then?'

'You know who.'

'Lady Risarial.' A pause. 'Where's your little human this time, eh?'

At the mention of Ruth, Risarial clenched her teeth, making fists with her hands so her vines wouldn't free themselves. She was right in front of the creature now, but she wanted to savour this.

'Lost your voice, eh?' the redcap said. 'Yeah, this place'll do that. You lost your power along with it? Make room for you in my home, I would. My bed. Room for that little dark thing of yours, too.' Low in her throat, the redcap chuckled.

One vine broke free and snaked around the redcap's wrists, pulling tightly enough that Risarial heard the snapping of bones. The redcap screamed, a low, gravelly sound that set Risarial's teeth on edge. To smother the noise, she wrapped a second vine around her neck.

Pulling the redcap tight against her, savouring the way her body twitched, the gurgling in her throat, she closed her eyes and thought of Ruth. When she'd awakened, cuffed to the chair, iron biting into her skin, she'd known that Ruth knew her for what she was. The relief of it, the horror. This whole time, she knew Ruth wasn't falling in love with her again, but for a moment, when she was raging at her, hating her, it had brought back the passion she had so loved about that angry, messy human. That was what she had come back for, that was her *Ruth*. And for the rest of her life, it would have to be enough.

She thought of the promise she broke, with equal parts regret and relief. Did the girl know the power she held over her now? A broken promise for the fae was not as it was for humans. She would be in Ruth's debt—and mercy— forever. She tightened her grip around the redcap's neck. Not like it mattered. Ruth never wanted to see her again and that was one promise she could keep.

Risarial gasped, her breaths coming quicker. How the redcap fought. She opened her eyes, wanting to see the moment that life fled the creature in her grip.

The redcap's eyes bulged and they looked left to right, seeking help, but none came. Some of them had probably left already—for the court, for home. Others stayed, wanting to watch the end of this grizzly match.

Risarial suddenly grinned when, with a satisfying thud, the bloody cap fell from the redcap's head onto the floor. Risarial slackened her grip and the creature fell too.

As she stood regaining her breath, someone went around the room lighting all the candles again. Her palms were bleeding and she rolled her neck, feeling the power of spilled blood running through her. Enough power to save a life with.

She looked around. The house was a hovel really, now she was inside. The room was dotted with sleeping mats and human clothes and whatever else they'd managed to amass in this forsaken place. There were suitcases lining the wall. Risarial walked over to them and flicked the lid of one. It was packed full of human money. Risarial huffed, shaking her head. How far they'd fallen. She closed the suitcase again and picked it up by the handle.

Catching the eyes of the few still in the room with her,

she said, 'The mist parts just after midnight.'

With nods and grateful bows, they scurried away, not wanting to miss what would most likely be their only chance to return home. It was more than they deserved but she needed them out of her way.

Risarial departed with them. She had one thing left to do before she too would return to the court.

❧ ❦

Risarial had never been inside a hospital before. The place was forbidden; that was drummed into them before they were even old enough to set foot earthside. They were places of exposure, of danger, of death to her kind. It made Risarial's skin crawl to be inside one now, but she wasn't there for herself, she was there for Ruth.

She went up to the first person she saw—an old woman with a walking stick and a black handbag far too big for her bony arms—and glamoured her to take her to the correct ward.

When she got there, no one paid her any mind. Nurses averted their eyes; patients saw nothing but a shadow, a smudge on the edge of their vision.

Sheila's room was at the end of the corridor. The blinds were shut against the bright late morning sunlight, casting the room into a warm dim. Risarial leant against the closed door for a moment, listening to the foreign sounds of machinery and getting used to the strange, chemical smell that permeated the whole building.

Her eyes were on the figure on the bed. She walked over and looked down, frowning at the shell lying there. Ruth's Sheila had always been a large woman, in body and in spirit, but now she seemed sunken.

Risarial cast her eyes over the room again. As a dying place, it was somewhat peaceful. She still fought the urge to shudder—dying wasn't something her kind did well.

She let out a breath. She couldn't be too long. She didn't

want to linger on the off chance that Ruth might choose this time to visit. Not like the girl would know who she was, but still.

Shrugging off the pang of heartbreak, Risarial leant over the bed. She flexed her hands, bringing forth the power of life the redcap had imbued onto her. With a hand on Sheila's forehead, she reached into the woman's body energy, lowering into the sick part of her. She grimaced as she probed—none of Sheila was particularly well. This world was just as poisonous for them as it was to her kind. It was definitely this woman's time to die.

She felt something akin to sludge and stopped. She let her glamour fall from her, her lips parting as the power crashed through her with full force. She swept away the sickness, eking it out of her, banishing it into that nether place.

When it was done, she stepped back, gathering her glamour around her again. She wouldn't stay well forever. The woman would return to her life, living as before, and the cancer would return. But not yet, not today. Ruth would never know, but she hoped it would ease her pain. Her last attempt at righting the wrongs.

As she peered through a gap in the blinds, where the sun glared, Risarial felt tears in her eyes.

It was time to go.

She turned and left the room, recalling the bargain she had made with her sisters. What a fool she was, to think the ending would be a happy one. She sniffed away the tears— it would be the final time she shed them. She would go home now and turn Cerulean out to this forsaken place.

She knew she wouldn't come back. This place was tainted for her now.

CHAPTER 25

Ruth pulled up the handbrake on Sheila's car, using her other hand to smother a yawn. It was late and she was tired and pissed off after another day of traipsing around looking for a job. Since the pub closed, she was even more fucked in terms of money. The tenancy on her flat had expired and Ruth calculated she had about three months' worth of rent left to her name so hadn't renewed it.

Jed had offered up his place. He spent a lot of time with the wild fae so she would have the flat to herself often, but Ruth declined. It just felt too close. Even the mere mention of fairies would cause her chest to constrict. It wasn't ideal, living in a car, but it would do until she got herself back on her feet. He had given her a key though.

Sighing, she tilted the seat back, eyes on the dark line of trees in front of her. She often found herself parking up at this carpark overnight. It was out of the way and wasn't used for anything as far as she could tell, not even during the day. No one had bothered her here yet, though she saw the occasional creature patter through the trees. Too large to be a fox or badger. They never paid attention to her sitting in the car and for that she was bloody glad.

They didn't know she could see them. She didn't have the Sight like Jed did, just the ability that the four-leafed clover gave her; to see through the veil. Sometimes she wished she couldn't see, and thought about throwing it out, returning to her ignorant existence like the rest of the world, but she just couldn't. She hated the thought of them being around her without her knowing, and on the one or two times she'd gone out without it, she'd spent the whole time eyeing up everyone they passed. The paranoia sucked.

She took out her phone. She'd have to drop it off at Jed's tomorrow to charge; the battery was almost drained. She brought up her browser, snorting at her last search—*do fairies have souls?*

She knew she was getting obsessed but she also knew herself well enough to know that that obsession was the only thing stopping her from falling into a dark hole she'd probably never get out of again. This was how she spent her nights—not sleeping, just trawling through sites and sites of fairy stuff. She knew she could ask Jed her questions but he was too much on their side and she found herself hating that. She wanted to hear answers from people like her—who were angry and scared. Who had been hurt by them.

Not a day went by that she didn't think about Ria. Was she back at the court now—eating plums and drinking goat's milk or whatever they bloody did when they weren't here fucking with humans? She thought about how her life would be now, if she hadn't been wearing the protective pouch and Ria had managed to take her memories again. At this point, she honestly wasn't sure which was preferable.

Ruth felt something knock the back of the car and she swivelled round, heart in her throat. Dropping her phone to her lap, she squinted. She couldn't see anything through the windshield and apart from a small LED lamp swinging from the wingmirror, everything was pitch black.

She held still, wrestling with the urge to turn off the lamp. She might not be able to see out but anything out there would be able to see her.

It was probably just an acorn or something, falling from the trees that hung over her car. She continued thumbing through her phone but she wasn't paying attention to the screen. Her body was tense like an animal's. If she didn't go out and check, she knew she'd never rest.

Drawing in a breath through her nose, Ruth sat up and unlocked the door. She planted her feet on the weed-speckled concrete and turned on her phone torch, waving it in an arc over the carpark. Nothing.

She got out of the car and rounded it, expecting some ugly goblin to jump out at her at any moment. There was something behind her car but it wasn't anything living. Ruth shined her torch downwards. It was a suitcase.

She looked at it for a moment before squatting down. It had definitely just been placed there—she would have felt a bump if she'd driven over it.

She cast her eyes over the empty carpark again. *Not suspicious at all.*

Cautiously, she reached out for the clasp. It was hard to undo with one hand but with a grunt, she managed to flip it. Leaning back as far as she could, she lifted the lid, her breath whooshing from her when she caught sight of its contents.

Along with the money, there was a rolled up note, tied with twine. With a sense of dread, Ruth picked it up and unfurled it.

From a stranger, to do as you wish. R.

'Oh, fuck off!' Ruth threw the note down, watching it bounce on the concrete where the edges fluttered in the nightly breeze. She stood up quickly, arcing the torch all around, trying to catch a trace of whomever had left it. But she knew there wouldn't be any.

She picked up the note, flung it back into the suitcase then grasped it by the handle. Damn Ria. She didn't want anything from that bitch yet Ria knew—she *knew*—Ruth wouldn't decline the money. She couldn't. She was living in a car for god sake, pissing in public bathrooms and brushing her teeth with her head hanging out the car door, spitting onto concrete.

She chucked the suitcase onto the passenger seat and turned off her phone torch. Her screen showed the last site she was on—some community forum for a place out in the sticks. Breathing hard from the outrage, she scrolled mindlessly, stopping at a random thread and clicking on it.

It was written by some girl. Ruth shook her head at the story before her—full of enchanted plant life and transforming faces. A couple of months back, she would have thought her whacky, the things she was saying, but now…

The post was a couple of months old. A few people had replied to it but it had petered out some weeks back. Ruth felt a shiver go through her at the girl's last line: *Can fairies take away your memories?*

Sitting up in excitement, Ruth clutched the phone tighter and with gritted teeth typed back, *Yes, they fucking can.*

TURN THE PAGE TO READ THE FIRST THREE CHAPTERS OF

❧ CERULEAN ❧

THE NEXT BOOK IN THE SISTERS OF SOIL SERIES.

CHAPTER 1

Elise took another drag from the cigarette balancing between two frigid fingers, trying her best to ignore the incessant quivering in her bones. The leaves beneath her shoes glittered with frost in the burgeoning sunlight and she stamped on them to warm her feet.

God, it was cold—and she was an idiot. She'd left her coat at the edge of the wood clearing so it wouldn't smell of smoke, but that wasn't doing much good for her now.

She huddled close to the fallen log behind her, drawing her bare legs to her chest. The sun was up, though only just, and everything was grey frost and morning shadow. Elise's heart bolstered. This was the time of day she lived for; it was this pathetic ritual that kept her days afloat.

The cigarette was nearly burnt down to the quick now. Elise curled her other hand against the washed-out black t-shirt, gleaning the meagre body heat from her stomach. It was her sister's, the t-shirt, not that she'd ever notice—she had about fifty of the things. Elise liked this one. It had a fairy printed in grey on it, albeit a scantily clad, outrageously posing one, but Elise had a thing for anything cute that might dwell in the forest.

Elise flicked the cigarette—she was getting good at that now—and the ash fell into her blonde hair, stark against the black of the t-shirt. She swiped the ash off and stood up, stamping the cigarette into the mud, a tiny little grave amongst others that she'd created in the last few weeks of

171

coming out here. Maddy would love that metaphor. Standing up, Elise frowned. She didn't want to be thinking about her sister.

With arms nearly too numb to function, she whipped the t-shirt off, rightening the cream coloured dress she had on underneath and feeling something close to resentment at the sight of it. Without the black t-shirt she was just Elise again—boring Elise, anxious Elise. The familiar heaviness settled around her again as she stuffed the t-shirt into a plastic bag and stuffed that in a crevice beneath the log.

Retrieving her coat, she began the walk back to the house, desperate to return to the warmth of it, but already mourning the girl she left behind in the graveyard of cigarettes.

She pulled the sliding patio doors open and blew out an audible breath at the heat of the kitchen before shrugging off her coat, tossing it over a stool. She glanced at the clock hanging from a beam then over at the bowl on the kitchen table—still untouched—and sighed. Crossing over to the kitchen counter, she picked up a box of cereal and slammed it next to the bowl before jogging up the stairs.

'Maddy!' She swung around the banister and knocked on her sister's door. She pushed it open, surprised it wasn't locked. 'Dude, get up.' The lump on the bed groaned and Elise rolled her eyes, slapping at it. 'It's Monday, Maddy, for god's sake. At least pretend to make an effort until midweek. You've got like twenty minutes before the bus. You can still make it.'

'I'll get the next one,' Maddy murmured, sticking her hands further under her pillow.

'I don't want to get that one. It gets in too late. Besides, you—'

'Oh my god, just get the bus on your own!' The mass of long hair on the pillow moved, twitching like a black octopus with its tentacles splayed. Maddy was always teasing her hair with her broken-toothed comb. Elise didn't know how she could run a brush through the tangled mess most days. 'Don't be such a baby.'

In the ensuing silence, Maddy sighed though it could hardly be heard over the sudden thudding of Elise's heart. 'Fuck you, Maddy,' she finally said.

Elise heard a mumbled *ouch* as she slammed the bedroom door shut. Back downstairs, she pulled on her shoes and coat, biting the inside of her lip against the anger. It wasn't enough to quell the anxiety, it never was, but it took the edge off. She left for the bus early; being the last one to board and fighting for a seat during Monday morning rush hour was literally the worst thing she could imagine.

It was too bloody cold. Elise sighed silently, curling her hand around her bus pass in her pocket, just to check it was there. She had some loose change too, just in case it got declined or whatever. So many just in cases. One day, Elise would love to just roll out of bed and stumble into life like Maddy seemed to do so bloody effortlessly. But then again, Maddy was a bit of a waster, so maybe not.

When the bus finally came, the increase in her heartrate was almost a relief, bringing some life back into her frozen body. She scanned the windows before the bus had even rolled to a stop. There were a couple of free seats. She relaxed slightly.

It was better on the bus. Once it got moving, she leaned her head against the window and put in her earphones, double-checking that they were plugged into her phone properly. A sound leak would be the death of her. She put on some heavier stuff this morning, trying to resurrect even an aura of the girl she'd left in the woods.

She was early to English, her first lesson, just how she liked it. She leant against the wall and slid down to sit on the floor of the corridor, music still trilling through her earphones. There was no one around so she turned it up and closed her eyes slightly, pretending she felt as carefree as she looked.

Maddy never came to English. Big surprise. As other students filed into the room, Elise rattled off a text and chucked her phone next to her textbook. *Idiot.*

She got a reply halfway through the lesson.

Maddy: Fell back to sleep, but on my way now, prommy x

CHAPTER 2

Maddy opened her mouth and executed a yawn, adding in some vocals to make it extra obnoxious. She scrubbed her watery eyes and leaned back in her chair. Her feet were drawn up to her chest, toes on the edge of the table, making the whole thing precarious.

'I'm wiped,' she murmured.

'Same,' the boy beside her replied, ruddy head held in a palm. Maddy glanced at Phil from the corner of her eye. He'd tried eyeliner this morning. He was getting better at it, but the flicks were too long. He tried to make them like hers, despite her telling him he just didn't have the eyes for it.

'Off we go then!' their lecturer said from the front of the class. Maddy roused herself along with the rest of the students, swinging her feet down from the table and picking up her camera.

They were off to take some pictures and despite the fact that she'd be freezing her tits off, Maddy didn't mind. Miles better than being holed up in the classroom.

They paraded down the street to where a weird sculpture-cum-climbing frame was. The rubbery ground was spongey under their feet and Maddy jumped up and down on it a couple of times to thaw out her numb extremities. Their lecturer began removing some balls from a bag—they were taking action shots today.

Maddy grabbed one then dragged Phil and his shitty eyeliner over to the edge of the area where they could doss around in peace.

'So, you gonna tell me about your date or what?' Maddy asked. They were both looking down at the screens of their cameras, altering the settings their lecturer had told them.

'Oh my god,' Phil began, voice conspiratorial, 'so don't be mad but I did something kind of fucked up.'

'Do tell.' Maddy found the right settings and pointed the camera at her classmates who were already throwing their balls around.

She liked hearing about Phil's nights out but since she wasn't eighteen yet, they made her kind of jealous too. Thank god her birthday was soon.

'So, you know Sandy Crack, the drag queen?' he said.

'Don't know her personally, but yeah.'

'Well, I gave her a BJ in the disabled toilets.'

Maddy lowered her camera. 'Isn't he, like, sixty?'

'Yeah, that's why it's so fucked! But I dunno, I was drunk and it wasn't that weird or anything.'

'*Okaaay,*' Maddy drew out. 'So what about this date?'

Phil waved his small, chubby hand. 'He bailed. We're rescheduling for next Saturday instead.'

'Fair.'

'You signed up yet?'

Maddy shook her head. Phil had signed up for whatever gay dating site he was part of before he'd turned eighteen but Maddy wanted to wait. She was kind of excited, nervous too, but would rather die than let Phil know that.

'Birthday's soon. Might as well wait. Besides, you said you'd set me up.'

Phil blew out a breath. 'Yeah, if there was anyone fit around here, which there's not. Believe me, I've been looking.'

Maddy snorted. 'Don't worry about it. Also, don't forget it's the party next Saturday. You can bring that boy but bail on me and I'll kill you.'

'Oh shit. Yeah don't worry, I'll do the date earlier in the day or something. Have you sent off for your provisional

ID yet?'

Maddy grimaced. 'Fuck. Not yet.'

'Get it sorted, idiot. No way are we not going out after the party.'

'I will, I will! Now shut up and go over there so I can take some pics of you throwing that bloody ball.'

CHAPTER 3

Cerulean arrived in the city at night, a sack slung over her shoulder that Risarial had hastily thrown together per her request. She knew her youngest sister had wandered here with nothing but her glamour, but Cerulean loved to make things easier for herself if she could.

The outer roads were like veins—narrow and quiet and threading in the direction of some eventual beating heart. Cerulean could smell life on the winter wind, hear its base deep beneath her feet. She followed the roads until they opened up into a vast, paved area, riddled with life. Her first thought was of an ant's nest, one she'd stamped on to rile up the minibeasts and send them running.

It was a night of revels and Risarial had told her most weeks were bookended with them. It was hard to know which to join—most doorways were teeming with humans, most wearing nothing but shocks of colour wrapped around their torsos and shoes with needle heels. Cerulean's nostrils flared. She'd been to a club once with her sisters but that time was different; she'd been there for Earlie and kept under the watchful gaze of Risarial. Now she was alone. Now she was free.

She took an alleyway that was bleeding with pink neon light. At the end of it, some human girls were bantering with a large blocky man. He had a smile on his wide face but his folded arms warded the girls away from whatever they were insisting.

On the floor at Cerulean's feet sat a man, a small dog curled in his lap. It turned its face up to Cerulean and gave a small bark.

'Shut it, Cassie,' the man snapped back. He said to Cerulean, 'Ah, she won't hurt yer. Just protective, that's all.'

Cerulean eyed the man with his tatty blanket and bearded face. She looked back at the neon club to see that the girls were now gone.

'You don't want to join the revel?' Cerulean asked the man.

'Eh?' He glanced at the club and chuckled. 'Back in my prime, back in my prime. They's friendly in there, them's lot. Always happy to stroke Cassie, aren't they Cassie?' The man lowered his face to the animal, the dog's tongue lapping at his chin like a lizard. It was vile. Cerulean grinned.

'You holing up somewhere?' the man asked, nodding at the bag slung over her shoulder.

'Excuse me?'

'You got a home or you begging?'

'Neither,' she said.

The man nodded. He looked up at her, shielding his eyes against the pink lights. 'Ah shit, I thought you was a man!' He chuckled again. 'Fuck me. Hey sweetheart, sorry to ask, but don't suppose you got any spare change on you? Don't ask for much. Just a coffee in the morning, maybe. Just a hot drink.'

Cerulean shrugged the bag from her shoulder and dropped into a squat beside it. Money was one of the things Risarial had packed for her, a whole wad of it, though she wasn't sure why. She could just as easily conjure the notes and coins herself.

She sat down next to the man, ignoring the low rumble from the dog. From her sack, she pulled out a twenty-pound note.

'Ah, I don't need that much, love.'

Cerulean regarded the note. She didn't have any smaller quantities. 'Would you like to gain it from me?'

'Eh?'

Cerulean folded the note up. It was plasticky, threatening to spring open against her palm. 'Answer me some questions and the money is yours. All is fair.'

After a moment of looking at her groggily, the man shrugged. 'Alright.'

'Which city is this?'

'Manchester, petal.'

Cerulean nodded. She had thought as much. She'd been here before though heavens knows which part of it.

'Do you know where I might find lodgings for the night?'

'I'm assuming you mean a hotel or something, not some piss-stained doorway?'

'Company would be preferable.' Cerulean smiled as two girls trotted by them.

'Eh?'

'It was hard being me, you know.' Cerulean kicked her long legs out, crossing them at the ankle. 'So many damn appearances to uphold. You wouldn't believe the amount of planning that went into visiting the bordello just the once. Absolutely not worth it, my friend. All that fawning.' Cerulean rolled her eyes. 'Heavens, I wish glamour worked on my own kind.'

'Sorry, I ain't following here.' The man turned, his face a mask of confusion. 'You asking me for a hotel or a brothel?' He squinted his eyes at her. 'You're one of those gays, aren't yer? You might want to try down by the canal there. Places for you there, a whole lot of them.'

'By the water?'

'Yeah, right. Follow the rainbow.' The man cackled. 'Can't steer you wrong, place is plastered with them flags.'

Cerulean clapped the man on the shoulder. 'I love a quest.' She slapped the note into his hands and stood up. 'May we meet again.'

✦

visit **hollythornebooks.com** to join the newsletter
and keep up to date with future book news!

✦

Printed in Great Britain
by Amazon

13648328R00108